REALITY TOUR

Thanks to the Circle of Christian Authors for your excellent input—and most of all, the constant encouragement. I cherish the ways each of you have contributed to my writing and to who I am becoming.

Reality Tour
Copyright © 2007 by G Studios, LLC

Requests for information should be addressed to:
Zonderkidz, *Grand Rapids, Michigan 49530*

Library of Congress Cataloging-in-Publication Data

Crouch, Cheryl, 1968-
  Reality tour / by Cheryl Crouch.
    p. cm. -- (Chosen Girls ; bk. 8)
    "G Studios."
    Summary: The Chosen Girls go on tour, but when Harmony's rebellious cousin Lucinda joins them, Harmony temporarily forgets the word of God in an effort to have fun and look cool.
    ISBN-13: 978-0-310-71274-9 (softcover)
    ISBN-10: 0-310-71274-2 (softcover)
    [1. Christian life--Fiction. 2. Bands (Music)--Fiction. 3. Cousins--Fiction. 4. Behavior--Fiction.]
I. Title.
    PZ7.C8838Re 2007
    [Fic]--dc22

                                                                    2007022890

Editor: Bruce Nuffer
Art direction and design: Sarah Molegraaf
Interior composition: Christine Orejuela-Winkelman and Melissa Elenbaas

Printed in the United States of America

07 08 09 10 11 12 • 7 6 5 4 3 2 1

REALITY TOUR

By Cheryl Crouch

ZONDERVAN.com/
AUTHORTRACKER
follow your favorite authors

Dear Miss Harmony Gomez,

You may know we're preparing for an upcoming youth campaign for the West Coast, called "Anything but Coasting." We've been looking for a fresh young California band that might tour with Jonah.

After reviewing everything from your band's lyrics, videos, and CDs, to the Christ-honoring reputation you've established, we feel that your band is just the group we want.

Would the Chosen Girls be interested in joining the "Anything but Coasting" tour? We'll hold sessions in San Francisco, Portland, and Seattle this spring. This youth campaign is

pray without stopping

PRAY

But you will receive power when the Holy Spirit comes on you; **and** you will be **my** witnesses in Jerusalem, and Judea and Samaria, and to the ends of the **earth.** —Acts 1:8

I'm hitting **the** road
Layin' down my load
Ready to have some fun!

→Finally **made** it big
   You should see my rig
We'll be cruisin' in the sun

We're the Chosen Girls
Touring the **coast**
We're the Chosen Girls

* Don't mean to boast ← Hee Hee Hee!
   We're the Chosen Girls
   And we're the **MOST!**

Ha Ha!

Con: over $4,000 to rent for a **week**

Pros:
Motor homes are so cute
I love **the** table that turns into a bed.

We just <u>have</u> to find a motor home!!

BUG on the Windshield

EEWWW!

Kill it!

Responsible

Minivans

Con: Have to stay **in** hotels

Pros: <u>No pros</u>

Airplane tickets

Con: No fun to come home each night

Pro: Mello doesn't have to miss school

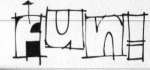

UPTOWN TROLLEY — One Passenger Ticket to Ride $5.00

* I love vacations!!!!
I love when **school** is finally out!
Cool frijoles!!!
and I know I don't have to use my brain for, like, a month or more.
OK, sí, I'll use **my** brain but not on tests or to write papers or **do** math.

Muy bueno!!!

Time to PARTY!!!!

SAN FRANCISCO

Come Visit

I wish I had a serious **camera** like the yearbook **camera**. Of course I have one on my cell and I **have** a cute litt**le** digital but if I blow up the pictures too big they're kind of grainy. And the **quality** isn't the best if I take the picture too close, either. I took one of M**ello** that makes her nose look HUGE. (She hates it.) Maybe I'll put a **new** camera on my Christmas list next **year**...

So Much Fun!

hiking!

FOR ME?!

Cool frijoles!!!

Don't let me be silent
When I have **so** much to say
Don't let me put it off
Till another day

* ◎ *

People need to know You
And all you have to give

If I hold Your life inside
Will others really live?

* ◎ *

Set Your words free
Let them flow from me
Share the good news
Don't want them to lose

order vs. disorder

I'm beyond psyched that Lucinda is joining us. My cousin Lucinda is way fun. We were like best friends when we were younger. I know that Mello and Trin will only (love) her. I wonder what my tia means that she is a "lost sheep." There must be a misunderstanding. She will love touring with the Chosen Girls!!!

Chosen Girls ROCK.

chapter • 1

...

When I was little, I made up stories about exotic places and amazing adventures. Sometimes, if I concentrated hard enough, reality faded away and my dream world took over. My bathtub became a flower-scented tropical pool, and the water rained down like a waterfall tumbling from a rocky cliff. And in my backyard, the pepper tree became a forest hideaway where I struggled to stay alive as the last survivor of my native tribe or Irish clan or Russian dynasty.

Always, my dreams were interrupted. "Armonia Aracelli Gomez, what's taking so long? There are six other people waiting for that bathroom!"

"Harmony, where are you? You haven't washed your dishes yet. Or taken out the trash. Or cleaned your room."

Anyway, that was when I was little. Now I'm growing up— practically grown. Between my rock band, school, karate, and family stuff, I've got loads of responsibilities. So I'm thinking it's time to stop dreaming about exotic places and amazing adventures, you know?

It's time to make those dreams come true.

• • •

I kicked open the door on the side of what used to be my best friend's family garage. Mello and I took over the building a long time ago, first as our playhouse and then as our studio. I'm not sure the McManns even once parked a car inside.

"Everybody here?" I called as I struggled to get my stuff through the door.

"Well, yeah," Trin answered. She sat half-sunk into the tan couch, arms folded, her brilliant trademark smile nowhere to be seen.

"We're all *still* here," Lamont said, raising his long brown arms and tapping his watch with a forefinger.

I glanced at Mello, already perched behind her drum set. She peered at me with one eyebrow cocked as if to say, "You're late for practice again, Harmony."

"I'm sorry, you guys," I answered. "And when you hear why I'm late, you'll understand that—"

"That you're a lame, lame excuse for a band manager?" Lamont said. I could see he fought back a smile.

"I'm serious, you guys. I have killer news," I said, dropping my gear and pulling a sheet of paper from my back pocket. I asked, "Do you know who Jonah Harrison is?"

"Jonah Harrison," said Trin matter-of-factly. "Everybody knows Jonah Harrison."

"Is he that new guy in your history class?" Mello asked.

"Get real," Trin answered. "He's a youth speaker."

"Not just a youth speaker," Lamont said. "Jonah Harrison is The Man. His 'We Are One' tour last year was huge. Twenty thousand in New York City alone."

Mello said, "Oh, right! I've heard of him."

"Of course you have," Trin agreed. "Everyone has."

"He doesn't just stand there and talk, right?" Mello said. "He travels with a band, and it's like a massive concert."

I nodded. "Sí. He drew in almost fifty thousand people between New York, Boston, and DC."

"Hey, I heard he's coming to L.A.," Lamont said. "It would so rock to hear him—"

"That's your news, isn't it, Harmony?" Trin interrupted, her eyes sparkling. "You got us tickets to his L.A. show!"

I shook my head and tried to look sad. "Nope. No tickets."

"No?" Mello said. "So why are we talking about him?"

I waved the email I had printed in front of them. "Because he wants us to join him on his next tour!"

"Backstage?" Trin yelled.

I laughed. "No. *Onstage.* The Chosen Girls will be his opening band."

They sat in stunned silence for a second, and then—

"Nuh-uh!" Lamont exclaimed.

Trin squinted at me. "You are *so* lying to us."

Mello just turned white.

I made a big deal out of smoothing the paper before I read aloud:

> Dear Miss Harmony Gomez,
>
> As you may know, we are preparing for an upcoming youth campaign for the West Coast, called "Anything but Coasting." We've been looking for a fresh young California band that might tour with Jonah.

After reviewing everything about your band, from your lyrics, videos, and CDs to the Christ-honoring reputation you've established, we feel that your band is just the group we want.

Would the Chosen Girls be interested in joining the "Anything but Coasting" tour? We'll hold sessions in San Francisco, Portland, and Seattle this spring.

I looked up. "After that it's a bunch of boring detail stuff about stage crews and travel expenses."

"You're serious, aren't you?" Lamont asked.

"Beyond serious," I answered. "The Chosen Girls can finally do a real tour. It's road trip time, amigos!"

We hugged and screamed and jumped around the room until Mello stopped and waved her hands at me. "Wait. What about school?"

"Checked that. The tour's during break," I answered. "Mostly, anyway. We'll just miss, like, two days."

"Mrs. Burledge won't like it," Mello said with a shake of her head.

Trin started pacing. "Ohwow, this is unreal. You're talking about *us*? Performing in front of maybe fifty thousand—"

"Touring the whole West Coast!" I yelled. "Portland, Seattle, San Francisco."

"With Jonah Harrison," Lamont added, rubbing his hands together.

"In an RV!" I continued. "I only love those little tables that turn into beds! And every little space has a drawer or cabinet tucked into it. Way beyond cute."

"I don't know," Trin mumbled. "It would be up to *us* to set the mood for Jonah's talk every single night. What we do would have a huge impact on the audience."

I smiled at her and propped my feet up on the coffee table. "Just think, Trin—no teachers, no schoolwork, no chores to do at home. Just cool places to explore and fans to amaze."

Trin sighed and looked at me. "Do you even realize what a huge deal this kind of tour would be? It wouldn't be a vacation, Harmony."

"You're right," I told her. "It would be better. Because someone else pays our way."

"Harmony—," started Mello.

"And it'll be just us. No parents! No one to remind us to do homework or—"

"So who would drive the RV?" Lamont asked. "And are you realizing how small that space is going to feel about halfway into the trip?" He looked us over. "Bands—even friendships—have fallen apart on tour before."

I rolled my eyes. "A six-month tour, maybe. This is three shows, Lamont."

Trin tossed a pillow to the floor and sat on it. "Let's think about this, Harmony. Are you sure our band is ready for—"

"Why should we wait?" I asked. "My favorite cousin, Lucinda, lives in Seattle. She is crazy fun, and she'd love to show us around. And Oregon is supposed to be way fabulous. We can hike and explore in the mountains and sightsee in the cities—"

"It's just bad timing," Mello said. "I'd feel better if it was during summer break. Besides, we've never done anything remotely—"

"Exactly!" I almost yelled. "We need something like this. And what does missing a couple of days of school matter compared to touring the coast?"

I felt my heart pounding. It hadn't even crossed my mind that they might say no.

"Listen," I said, toning my voice way down. "This is the chance of a lifetime." I looked at the serious faces around me and wondered how they could want anything besides this opportunity.

I'd assumed even Mello—who's usually scared to try something new—would see what this could do for our band. And Trin—come on—Trin's always up for doing something big. Was she actually afraid that this was *too* big?

Even Lamont with the relationship thing? Please! We'd already been through every traumatic experience a band could face. What could possibly happen *now* to break up the Chosen Girls?

"Please tell me you're in," I begged.

Lamont crossed his arms. "I think we'd have to have some major rules—"

"Sure," I agreed. "You know me. I'm, uh, all for rules."

"We'd have to pick up our schoolwork ahead of time—," Mello began.

I smiled at her. "Of course. And we can help each other while we're on the road."

"But most of all, the concerts would have to be priority, Harmony," Trin insisted. "I agree that we should have some fun, but we can't let Jonah down, and we can't disappoint all the people who will be showing up looking for hope and direction."

I said, "Well, yeah. All those people who need to hear what our band stands for—we'll reach more of them than ever before. Isn't that cool?"

Trin *finally* smiled her megawatt smile. "Yeah, it is. Ohwow, it's way cool. We could make a real difference."

I looked at Lamont.

He nodded and a grin spread across his face. "Gotta admit, yeah, it's an amazing opportunity."

I bit my lip and turned to face Mello. "What do you think?" I asked.

She let out a huge breath. "Performing in front of all those people? It's terrifying. And I hate missing school. It'll take me forever to catch up, even if it is just a couple of days." Then her eyes started to twinkle, and she finally smiled. "But, really, how could we say no?"

•••

After practice, I rushed home to tell Mamma. Papi would be excited too, but he was traveling for work, so I'd have to call him.

"Look, Mamma!" I yelled as I burst into the kitchen. I slapped the email onto the counter beside the cutting board.

She glanced up from the yellow squash she was slicing. "What is it?"

"The Chosen Girls are invited to tour with Jonah Harrison!" I spun around, unable to contain my joy. "We leave in a month!"

I held my arms out to her, ready to receive a congratulations hug.

She stepped into my arms and squeezed me back, but it didn't feel like much of a congratulations hug. Especially when she said, "Oh, I'm sorry, Harmony. I don't think it's going to work out."

I pulled away from her. "What? How can it not work out?"

"Something big has come up, and I need to discuss it with you," she said, wiping her hands on a dish towel.

I dropped into a chair, heart racing, imagining a million reasons why we might have to call off the tour. "What is it?"

"Aunt Berta called about your cousin Lucinda."

"Weird. I was just telling *mis amigas* how she's my favorite cousin. Is she OK?"

"She's been kicked out of school."

"No way. What did she do?"

"Berta didn't say."

"It's got to be some kind of misunderstanding," I told her.

Mamma shook her head. "Berta is very concerned about Lucinda. It seems she's making a lot of bad choices."

I gulped. "Like what?"

"I didn't ask for details, Harmony. Berta kept crying, calling Lucinda her 'lost sheep.' She wants to send Lucinda to us. She's hoping your influence will turn her around."

"Great. She can come now, and we'll have almost a month together before the tour."

Mamma paced in front of me. "That's the problem. Lucinda has to go to hearings or something this month. Berta wants to send her to us next month. I'll need you here—not running around the country."

"That's not fair!" I exclaimed, jumping out of my chair. "If Lucinda wants to mess up her life, that's her deal. But I'm not going to let her wreck mine too."

Mamma put her hands on my shoulders. "That's not the way it works in a family, Harmony. Lucinda's choices affect all of us. And she needs you now to make a hard choice—the right choice—so you can have a good effect on her."

I kicked at the linoleum floor. "There has to be a way," I mumbled, my brain in hyperdrive. "What if she comes on the tour with us? We'll end up in Seattle, Mamma. It's perfect! She'd get to hear Jonah speak. What could be better? I know she'll adore Mello and Trin, and they'll love her. They won't be able to help themselves—she's crazy fun."

Mamma looked unsure.

"Please, Mamma," I begged. "At least ask Aunt Berta. This tour means the world to me."

Mamma sighed. "So you're willing to be responsible for her? To see that she doesn't get into trouble, cause any problems?"

"Sí. I'm not just willing, I'm beyond psyched," I answered.

Mamma said, "All right, then. I'll call Berta and see what she thinks of the idea."

I rushed out of the kitchen and upstairs to my room, planning to IM Mello, Trin, and Lamont with the news. Then I changed my mind. They already had enough reservations about the tour. Did I really want them worrying about my rebellious cousin too?

Better wait to mention Lucinda until I knew her plans for sure. In the meantime, we could all focus on getting ready for the trip of a lifetime.

chapter • 2

...

Saturday, one week Later

The next Saturday we went to find a vehicle for our big road trip. At the rental place, we checked out a few of the nicest RVs—the kind with sides that pop out to make the living room bigger and cameras in the rear so the driver can back up safely.

"I only love this!" I said as we poked around in the third one. "The shower is way beyond tiny!"

"And that's supposed to be a good thing?" Trin asked.

Mello squeezed past Trin and peeked in the bathroom. Then she winked at me. "I can see why Trin's worried. I don't think that head of hair she's got will even fit in there."

"Whatever!" Trin responded. "You so have more hair than I do, Mello."

"Maybe yours just looks bigger because of that neon shade of pink," Lamont offered. "It's, uh, highly visible. Kind of like an emergency flare."

"I'll choose to take that as a compliment," Trin answered. She sat on the edge of the bed in the compact master bedroom.

"Hey, don't get too comfortable on my bed," I warned.

She laughed. "*Your* bed?"

"Isn't it understood that the band manager gets the biggest bedroom?"

Trin made a big show of stretching out. "You wish! It's totally reserved for the lead singer."

"Ooh! Put the diva's star on the door," I crooned.

"I guess as drummer and backup singer I have no claims," Mello said. "But Harmony, you're on the table, remember?"

"What?"

She squatted down to look under the table next to the couch. "Didn't you say you love these tables that turn into beds? This one does, I can tell."

"I adore the *concept* of a table that turns into a bed," I explained as I turned around and leaned against the countertop. "I mean, how cute is that? But I don't love actually *sleeping* on a table that has turned into a—"

Trin opened the closet door and screamed.

I jumped, and Mello tried to stand up and bumped her head on the underside of the table.

Lamont rushed back to the bedroom. "What is it?"

"Ohwow, it's this closet! It could hold maybe three outfits, max. I've seen shoe boxes bigger than—"

"OK, Trin, that was very uncool," Lamont scolded. "I run back here ready to rescue you from some kind of wild beast in the closet and—"

"But look in there!" she insisted. "Packing is going to be a serious issue."

"But that's what's fun-o-rama about an RV!" I said. "We don't really even have to pack. We just move in! No suitcases to haul around—"

"Trin is right, though," Mello said. "We're not going to be bringing much. That means you both need to get a handle on your shoe issues."

"What shoe issues?"

"The bizarre need you both have to take at least seven pairs of shoes along any time we're gone overnight. I don't think we'll be able to fit more than a couple of pairs each in here. And only one artsy-craftsy project each, looks like," said Mello.

I looked at Trin, who appeared ready to hyperventilate. "Don't panic. We'll stuff a few pairs of shoes between the instruments in Lamont's truck."

"Good thinking," Trin said, bonking fists with me.

Lamont shook his head. "Hey now, I'm the one who's gonna be crammed in some sorry pop-up trailer while you're in here chillin' with the big screen. Don't be trying to slide your stuff into my ride."

"But we have to take a lot, Lamont," Trin said. "We're rock stars. We have an image to maintain."

"So true," I agreed. "You don't want all those TV reporters filming us in the same clothes day after day, do you?"

He nodded. "I hear ya. Since I'm only the lowly soundman, no one cares what—"

"It's not that," Trin hurried to say. "It's just that you don't have to try as hard as we do."

"Well, yeah. You have a point there," Lamont agreed, stroking his chin. "My natural good looks come through no matter what I wear, you know what I'm saying?"

Mello rolled her eyes. "Seriously, guys, it's not going to be easy to make this work."

I waved my hands around at the small space. "But isn't it way adorable? It feels so cozy!"

Mello sighed. "Yeah, I guess cozy is one way to describe it. If we can live together in this tin can, our friendship will survive anything."

"Exactly!" I agreed. "We're in for some serious bonding. I can just see us gathered around this little table playing Scrabble—"

"Scrabble?" Trin called from the other room.

"What's wrong with Scrabble?"

"You have to think too hard. And I reek at spelling."

"Fine, then. I can see us around this table playing Dutch Blitz—"

Mello interrupted. "I can't stand Dutch Blitz. Those games where you have to be the fastest one—they make me crazy. No way can you have a conversation or even let an idle thought float through your—"

I blurted out, "So I don't know what game we're playing. Fine. But in my mind I can see us, I tell you, plain as day. And we're sitting around this very table, and we're having fun! And no one is complaining or whining or griping about whatever the particular activity is and—"

Lamont ran his hand over his cropped black hair. "That pop-up trailer is sounding better and better."

I tapped the table with my pointer finger. "And I think this is where it's going to happen. Right here. Don't you think it's the best RV of all of them?"

Lamont stretched his long, thin legs across the couch. "I don't know. I liked the first RV better. It had a bigger TV."

"But you're going to be crammed in the sorry pop-up, remember? Besides, this one has pink curtains," Trin said, finally coming out of the master bedroom.

I rolled my eyes at her. "Oh, that's it, then. We have to choose the one that matches Trin's hair." I took one last look around the inside of the motor home. "Come on, everybody. Let's go pick up the rental agreement on this baby."

•••

"It's *how much*?" Trin screeched at the salesman.

He didn't even flinch, and his brown eyes gazed steadily out from behind thick glasses as he repeated, "Four thousand, two hundred dollars."

"But we only want it for a week or two," I explained. "We don't want to buy it."

That got a reaction. He laughed so hard he had to take off his glasses and wipe tears from his eyes.

When it appeared he'd never stop laughing, I started feeling irritated. "OK, look, I know that wasn't the sale price. How much does one of those sell for, anyway?"

He breathed in deeply through his nose and put his glasses back on. "That particular model goes for three hundred thirty thousand dollars."

Lamont whistled.

"So that price you quoted—the four thousand—that gets it for how long?" I asked.

"One week. Seven days. And, of course, you pay for gas."

Trin stood up. "Well, thank you so much for your time. We need to check all our options before we make a decision."

Mello and Lamont followed her to the door.

I forced myself to smile at the man as I said, "We'll be back."

The price scared me, but out in the parking lot my dream of our ultimate vacation really began to crumble.

"No way can we afford that thing," Mello said. "We're gonna have to, like, look at minivans or something."

"Minivans?" I shrieked. "I am not pulling up to Candlestick Park in a mom-mobile."

Trin pulled out her PDA and started punching in numbers. "It probably makes more sense to fly to each venue. Besides, that would save us—what? Forty-eight hours on the road, at least."

"We might not even have to miss school that way," Mello added.

Lamont nodded. "And flying would give you a better chance of coming out of the deal still liking each other too."

"You're forgetting the bonding potential on the road, Lamont," I said. "All that time will bring us together like never before. Besides, if we fly, we still have to come home and do homework and laundry and go to karate and all that boring real-life stuff. Where's the sense of adventure in that?"

Trin raised her eyebrows. "Loads of people might think flying to another city and rocking out in front of thousands of people is an adventure, Harmony."

"Way more adventure than I ever planned on," Mello agreed.

"Yeah, yeah," I admitted. "But I want to explore new places and make memories together and, you know, get away. Not just for a day or two. I'm beyond burned out on normal day-to-day stuff."

Mello put an arm around my shoulders. "I understand where you're coming from, Harmony. I've been there. Definitely. But if it costs too much, what can we do?"

"Did you forget that the letter said they'd cover expenses?" I asked. "They just asked us to be responsible, since it's a ministry and funds are tight."

She gave my shoulder a squeeze. "Right, Harmony. They're trusting us to make good decisions."

"Well, you can't tell me we'd be money ahead paying for four round-trip tickets to three different places."

"She might be right. And don't forget the fees to fly all your equipment," Lamont added. "You've got some serious extra baggage."

Mello said, "That's true. Even without Trin's and Harmony's shoes."

Trin growled and punched a button, hard. "Hush! I can't think when you're all chatting it out. I've got to start over again adding this up." While she punched she said, "If we got round-trip tickets to each place for four hundred, that'd be sixteen hundred for all four of us. Times three places, that's—"

She waited for the total and announced, "Forty-eight hundred dollars."

I smiled triumphantly. "Ha! And that's if we could get tickets that cheap, which I doubt we could. Besides extra baggage. So the RV *is* less."

"But the minivan would be even cheaper," Mello countered. "And gas—how much would gas set us back in that monster?"

"So now the RV is a monster?" I asked. "You're calling our cozy little home away from home—"

"I'm just saying—"

Trin started punching buttons again. "If we got a minivan, we'd have to pay driver's fees, plus hotel rooms each night."

"Good point, Trin. And meals. Three meals a day for each of us—add another, what? Hundred or so a day. But in the RV we can cook our own food. Think how much money we'll save."

"Isn't cooking one of those boring, real-world things you want to avoid?" Trin asked, looking up at me.

"On that sweet little stove? It will be like playing house. Oh, and you'd better double that hotel bill. We'll need three rooms a night, if we take our soundman along."

"If?" Lamont demanded. "If? Since when is my attendance an optional—"

I punched him on the shoulder. "I'm messing with you, Lamont. Calm down."

"Be careful, now," he said. "You know that's not funny. Nobody appreciates the soundman. Nobody even notices the soundman unless something goes wrong."

"We appreciate you, Lamont," Trin promised. "Without the music videos you make of us, we'd probably still be just another garage band—"

"Messing around in the shed," I continued.

Mello patted him on the back. "Instead of an award-winning band—"

"Heading out on a West Coast tour!" I squealed. Trin and Mello joined me as we jumped around in a happy little circle.

Lamont put his head in his hands. "Remind me why I even *want* to come along on this trip."

"My dad knows some people," Mello offered after we settled down. "They've got an RV almost as big as that one. They're really into ministry too. I don't know, maybe we could work something out with them."

I hugged her, hard. "You're brilliant, Mello! And I love your father and the fact that he knows, like, everyone in California. This is our answer. I just know it!"

Mello backed away. "Don't get too excited, Harmony. I have no idea if—"

"Just talk to your dad," I insisted. "Immediately. And start ordering brochures on RV camps and tourist sights. Lamont, get on your computer and start planning our route. Estimate time and how much gas we'll need. Trin, do some research on how to pack efficiently and find recipes for meals that will be easy to make."

I rubbed my hands together in anticipation.

"And you will—," Trin prompted.

"I'll start getting some board games together," I offered. "And *plenty* of chocolate."

chapter • 3

...

Sunday Afternoon, a week Later

"Mello, I knew your dad would come through!" I said as we stood on the Capagios' porch and waited for them to come to the door.

"Well, it's our turn to come through now," she answered. "This is a huge responsibility." She stopped talking as the front door opened.

A smiling woman with gray-streaked hair held the door for us. "Hello, girls. Come in, come in. I'm Theresa Capagio, and of course you're Trin and Mello and Harmony. You'll have to straighten me out on who's who. But I can guess who this fine-looking young man is! You must be Lamont."

We followed her into an immaculate living room decorated very simply but tastefully in browns and blues. A short man with a sizable potbelly met us there.

"This is my husband, Renaldo. You can call us Mr. and Mrs. C," she said with a smile. "Renaldo will explain all about the RV. It's a complicated piece of machinery, let me tell you. I must admit, some of it is beyond my understanding. So I'll just listen in while he tells you everything you need to know. Here, sit down. Sit down."

We found seats and Mrs. C disappeared.

"I'm sorry my wife and I can't drive you," Mr. C began.

Mrs. C's voice floated in from another room. "Wait, dear. Don't start yet. I'm just getting some lemonade for our guests."

He shrugged and grinned at us, and a minute later she came back with a tray of filled glasses.

After serving everyone, she said, "All right, dear. Go ahead."

"As I was saying, we'd love to drive you ourselves, but—"

Mrs. C jumped in. "It's simply impossible. You see, we've already committed to a mission trip in Brazil during that time. But the good news is, our RV is available for your campaign."

"We appreciate you letting us use it," Trin said.

Mr. C smiled at us. "When Mello's father explained that your band has been—"

"Invited to travel with Jonah Harrison!" Mrs. C exclaimed. "What an honor! And what an opportunity to share the good news of God's love. We're just so pleased to offer our RV to you for this ministry. But there really are some very important things to know about an RV. If you don't pay attention, you can do some serious damage, can't you, dear? Why don't you tell them about it?"

"Well, you've got to—"

"That's why we wanted to go along, you see," she said. "Then Renaldo could be sure everything is looked after properly. Not that we don't trust the Thompsons, of course. I'm sure they'll be careful, won't they, dear?"

"I'm so glad you found the Thompsons to drive for us," I said. "None of our parents could get away for the whole time, and—"

Wrinkles fanned out from Mrs. C's eyes as she smiled at me. "You'll love the Thompsons. Wonderful people—salt of the earth. Of course your father knows them well, Mello, or I'm sure he wouldn't let you go traipsing across the country with them. And they are just thrilled about the trip. They're big supporters of Jonah Harrison's ministry. On top of that, they've always wanted to drive up the West Coast. So you see, it's a beautiful opportunity for them as well." She looked at her watch. "Now, Renaldo, I'm sure these fine young people have better things to do today than sit around and listen to two old people. Why don't you tell them some of the things to watch for on the RV."

"One of the main things is to keep an eye on your gas gauge," he said. "The generator—"

"Oh, heavens yes," Mrs. C interjected. "Renaldo watches that gas gauge as if his life depended on it! Something about how it affects the generator, isn't it, dear?"

"Exactly. You see, if the gas gets below a quarter tank, the generator shuts off and then—"

"Well, you simply have no power, and at that point you can't just get more gas and solve the problem," Mrs. C explained. "What a headache! You know, we Americans have gotten so used to our electronic gadgets! We simply can't function without them. Of course that's the big advantage of an RV over a tent or some of your more basic travel trailers. I daresay I couldn't last twenty-four hours in a tent!" She looked at her watch again. "You'd better get on with it, Renaldo. These young people may have somewhere to go tonight."

Mr. C cleared his throat. "Of course, most people are concerned about how the holding tank works."

"A very delicate topic of conversation, I'm afraid," Mrs. C commented. "Still, it must be addressed. You certainly don't want anything going wrong with the toilet, now, do you? Tell them about it, Renaldo, dear."

So Renaldo Dear told us about the toilet. And keeping the cabinet doors closed. And limiting the amount of water we used. And on and on—all with plenty of help from Mrs. C, of course.

I whispered to Mello, "Enough information. When do we get to see this thing?"

She narrowed her eyes and shushed me, hanging on every word they said as if it were the most interesting lecture she'd ever heard.

I tried Trin. "Won't the Thompsons be taking care of all this stuff?" I asked. "Why do we need to know it?"

Trin shrugged and whispered, "If they want to tell us, we need to listen."

I sighed and sat back in the couch, dreaming about all the cool things we'd get to do on our trip. I'd already done some Internet searches on San Francisco. I could hardly wait to ride a cable car and shop at Union Square—or maybe we should hit Fisherman's Wharf. The San Francisco Zoo also sounded way fabulous, and of course we couldn't miss the Golden Gate Bridge.

Portland would be a completely different kind of cool. Portland seemed to be all about nature and art. It's close to mountains, desert, and ocean—and I wanted to see all of it. I hoped the flowers would be blooming when we got there, because they're supposed to be amazing. Maybe we could even hike partway up Mount Hood. I wasn't sure how Mello would react to a hike, but maybe if we balanced it out with a visit to an art museum—

Mr. C stood up. "So let's head on out and meet Bessie," he said.

"Bessie? Is that Mrs. Thompson's name?" Trin asked.

Mrs. C started gathering up our glasses. "No, Bessie is our name for the RV. And it's about time you stopped talking and showed it to them, dear," she told her husband. She smiled her crinkly eyed smile at me and asked, "Have you ever known a man to talk like he does? I was afraid he'd never finish up."

Finally! I shook myself free of my daydreams and followed everyone out the back door. The RV sat on a cement slab, basically filling their whole backyard.

"It's not as big as the ones we toured," I whispered.

"It's also not costing four grand," Lamont reminded me.

I made myself ignore the huge scratch between the front and back windows and followed Mr. and Mrs. C inside. "Does that table by any chance—"

"It turns into a bed!" Mrs. C declared. "Isn't that just adorable? Here, I'll show you how it works."

The inside of the RV was a little worn, but it still had a master bedroom, kitchen, bathroom, and living area complete with a TV and DVD player. Not bad for free.

We'd just finished up the tour when I heard, "Yoo-hoo. Anybody home?"

"Oh! It's the Thompsons," Mrs. C said. "Isn't this lovely? You'll get a chance to meet each other."

She hustled us out to the yard. "These are the Thompsons—Sandie and Bob. And Bob, Sandie—meet the Chosen Girls!"

Sandie Thompson's bright blue eyes twinkled from her chubby face as she walked toward me. I held out my hand for a handshake, but she ignored my hand and wrapped me in a bear hug. "So glad to meet you!"

Before I had a chance to respond, she moved on to hug Trin. "You precious, precious girls! Singing for our Jesus!" She wiped tears away and reached for Mello, who stood at least a head taller than she did. "Don't tell me you're the McMann girl. Why, the last time I saw you, you were just a tiny thing dressed in ribbons and lace—still in diapers!"

Mello tried to smile but didn't quite succeed.

"And you must be our soundman," Sandie continued as she took Lamont into her short, pudgy arms. "Isn't it beautiful to see young people using their skills for God, Bob?"

I had forgotten about Bob. We all turned and saw him standing tall about ten feet away, sinewy arms crossed, weathered face unsmiling. He offered a minimal nod.

"Hello, Mr. Thompson," I croaked. "Thank you for driving us."

Again, the slightest movement of his head.

Mrs. C said, "Well, Bob and Sandie, I'm so glad you're here. What a fantastic opportunity to work out the details!

Wouldn't this be a great time to divide up the chore list, Renaldo, dear? We can go back in the house to do that."

"Right. Let's—"

"Chore list?" I asked in surprise. I had planned on leaving the chore list far behind in Hopetown. Wasn't that the point of getting away?

Mrs. C smiled at me. "Well, of course. Why do you think Renaldo went over all that information with you? It's going to be up to you girls to take care of our Bessie."

"I'm a little ditzy when it comes to mechanical things," Sandie confessed with a shake of her head. "Just not the way God gifted me, I'm afraid. Bob is capable, of course, but he'll be driving the truck."

"And it seems fair for you to help," Mrs. C added before heading to the house. "It will be a way to earn your keep, so to speak."

"Oh, Theresa!" Sandie exclaimed, covering her mouth as if she were embarrassed by the very thought of us doing chores. "These sweet children don't need to earn their keep! For heaven's sake, they're going forth to sow gospel seeds."

While I didn't love being called "sweet children," I did love that someone realized we wouldn't have time for work. I was quick to agree. "We will be awfully busy with the concerts and—"

For the first time, Bob spoke. His deep voice rumbled like thunder. "If they ain't willin' to help, then I ain't takin' 'em."

Trin shot me a nasty look and said, "Of course we'll be happy to do anything that needs to be done."

"Right. We're not afraid to work hard," Mello added.

Lamont smiled at Bob. "My dad has taught me quite a bit about vehicles, and Mr. C here gave us the lowdown on Old Bessie. We'll do a good job."

I wanted to say, "Speak for *yourself*. I'm going on *vacation*." But we needed this RV, and we needed these people to drive us. So instead I smiled at Bob. "What I meant to say was, even though we'll be extremely busy with concerts, somehow we'll find time to do whatever you need us to do."

Bob's expression gave me the feeling he was sizing me up and wasn't at all impressed. I turned to Sandie instead, who wiped more tears from her cheeks. "What willing spirits! God is going to use your band in a mighty way."

Mr. C gestured toward the house. "Why don't we go back in and—"

"Renaldo, dear," Mrs. C called from the porch. "Don't keep everyone outside all day, for heaven's sakes. You can talk just as well inside."

Back in the house, the Capagios actually got out paper and made a big chart to divide up the jobs—whose turn to check the holding tank, watch the gas gauge, wash the dishes, sweep out the RV . . .

I started to feel like I might be better off staying home. To keep from getting discouraged, I imagined ways to trick out our new ride. It wouldn't cost much, I figured, if I designed a way cool slipcover for the couch and got Mello to sew it up. And, of course, we'd need hot pink curtains for the diva's room, and maybe some trippy throw pillows.

"Harmony, are you OK with this rotation for cooking and washing up?" Trin asked.

"Sí," I answered. "Looks great."

I wondered about a black light for the living area. How fun would that be? We could put on white gloves and make up glow-in-the dark choreography.

Or would a disco ball be even better? I only loved the thought of little rainbows of light spinning over and around us. *Cool frijoles*, I thought. *Old Bessie isn't gonna know what hit her.*

"You all understand about the holding tank?" Mr. C asked.

"No worries," I assured him.

Now, what about the outside of the RV? It's not like we could afford dent removal and a paint job. How could I make sure people would gape in awe as we cruised the super slab?

I could get one of those magnet signs! Of course. I'd seen pizza delivery chains use huge posters made from magnets that could stick to the side of trucks, cars, whatever. A big enough Chosen Girls logo could cover that dent and draw some serious attention at the same time.

"All right, then, I think that just about wraps it—," Mr. C began.

"Renaldo, dear, if you're about finished, I'm sure these young people have places to go and things to do," Mrs. C said. "And hasn't this been a lovely afternoon? I can see that everything is going to work out splendidly, don't you agree, Sandie? Bob?"

Sandie cried tears of joy and offered her heartfelt agreement.

Bob inclined his head about a quarter of an inch.

chapter • 4

...

Wednesday Night, a Week and a Half Later

I hadn't quite finished my redecorating job when the others showed up at the RV, so I locked myself inside and yelled, "Don't come in. I'm working on a surprise."

Trin called, "How long will it take?"

I pushed the curtain rod through the last pink curtain and hung it in place. "I just need a few more minutes."

"We kinda need to move this stuff in," Mello said. "That's why we're here, remember?"

I put double-stick tape on the back of a gold poster-board star and pressed it onto the door to the bedroom. "Not much longer. And you're going to love this, for reals."

I heard Lamont at the door. "Harmony, it's getting late, and we're pulling out early tomorrow. I want to get this done and go home."

"So load the truck," I answered, straightening the slipcover on the couch and quickly tossing the throw pillows onto the bed.

"Been there, done that," he answered.

I centered the tabletop disco ball on the table, stretching the cord to the nearest outlet. Now our RV looked like the ultimate vacation getaway machine. I unlocked the door and said, "OK, count to three and then come in."

As Trin pushed the door open, I turned on the light. The rainbows danced over the ceiling and across the Chosen Girls posters I'd put on the walls.

"Ohwow!" Trin yelled. "Ohwow, ohwow, get in here, Mello!"

Mello climbed in and her jaw dropped. "How did you—"

"Not bad," Lamont said as his head popped through the doorway.

"You got a new couch," Trin exclaimed. "And filmy swag curtains and—"

"And the fluffiest rug." Mello smiled at me as she bent down to run her fingers over the blue plush material.

Lamont fingered the bead curtain that hung between the driver's section and the living room. "Very . . . retro. Cool."

Trin squealed, "You actually made a star!" She opened the door to the bedroom and screamed, "Pink curtains! I've got pink curtains. For this, I may actually let you sleep on the big bed sometimes."

Mello hugged me. "Harmony, it's amazing! How did you keep all this secret?"

"At first I was going to ask you to help," I admitted. "But I decided it would be way more fun to surprise you instead."

Trin hugged me next. "You're beyond fabulous, Harmony! We are *so* going to have fun in here."

I hugged her back and said, "You got that right!"

"Yeah, well. Be thinking about me," Lamont said. "I'll be chillin' in the pop-up with Bob."

Trin snickered. "Come on, Lamont. Bob looks like a real bundle of fun."

"Sure. Hey, that reminds me. Did anyone get tissues for Sandie?" Mello asked.

"Got them," I answered. "Although we may have to restock before Portland."

"Just don't say anything touching," Trin suggested.

Lamont laughed. "Good luck with that. I bet she cries during Hallmark commercials."

Mello grinned. "Lamont, that woman probably cries during cereal commercials."

"So now we can move in, huh?" I asked.

Mello smiled and looked around the newly redone space. "Definitely. And now I *want* to move in."

"I'll stand here at the table and check in each item," Trin said.

I squinted at her. "What do you mean, 'check in'?"

"To make sure no one's sneaking stuff that's not on the list," she answered, pulling a folded sheet of paper from her pocket.

"Trin, isn't that a little extreme?" Mello asked. "Don't you trust us?"

Trin pulled out a pen and got ready to mark things off. "Look, I'm in charge of efficient packing. I'm just doing my job."

Lamont said, "But Trin—"

"Hey! If I'm limiting myself to three pairs of shoes, everyone's limiting themselves. If you followed the rules on the paper I gave you last week, we shouldn't have any problems. Start bringing your stuff."

Mello shot me a worried look as we stepped out of the RV. "Why did you put her in charge of packing?"

"I didn't know she'd take it this seriously," I answered as I grabbed my first load.

Mello sighed loudly. "Harmony, this is Trin we're talking about."

"Right. I should have known."

Lamont laughed as he walked past us. "And the fun begins."

"Shampoo?" Trin asked as she dug through Mello's box back at the RV. "What are you trying to pull here?"

Mello looked down, the very picture of a criminal caught red-handed.

Trin waved the offending bottle in the air. "We can take one bottle of shampoo between us. Period. And we voted to take Latheré with conditioner. It will save space and time."

I sang the Latheré jingle. "One quick minute, one easy step."

Mello wasn't impressed. "And *I* told *you* I can't use shampoo with conditioner. My hair will be a grease pit, Trin. Lighten up. For heaven's sake, it's a travel-size bottle! Three-point-five ounces!"

Trin shook her head. "Three-point-five ounces here, a pound of something there—next thing you know we're riding on top of the RV because there's no room for us inside. I'm sorry, Mello, really. I know we all have our favorite brand of everything from lotion to deodorant. I, for one, can't stand that cinnamon-flavored toothpaste you and Harmony voted for. But I'm going to use it for the good of the group."

She put the shampoo aside and continued to dig. Thankfully, the shampoo proved to be Mello's only transgression.

My box was a different story.

"Wool socks? Where do you think we're going—Alaska?"

I crossed my arms in defiance. "My feet always get cold at night. I can't sleep without warm socks."

Trin continued to pull stuff out. "You can wrap your feet in T-shirts. And *five* pairs of shoes! You thought I wouldn't notice that?"

"But three pairs are sandals! Together, they take up less space than your boots."

Trin spread the shoes on my fluffy blue rug. "Three pairs of shoes, total. Choose them now. The others stay behind."

I growled as I put my purple flip-flops and white sandals beside the wool socks.

"Tell me this is not really what it says on the box," Trin said, holding up another item I'd wanted to surprise them with.

"I know! Isn't it too fun? Our very own chocolate fountain. Can't you just see us after a big concert coming back to the RV and—"

"No, I can't," Trin insisted. "There were no chocolate fountains on the packing list, Harmony. And no—what is that? A hot-air popcorn popper?"

"Sí! Air-popped is so much healthier, and it's fun to watch it come out the little chute deal as it—"

"Sorry. We'll be eating microwave popcorn."

I finally lost it when she vetoed my bottle of sparkling cider and fancy stemware to drink it from. "Trin, you're worse than a guard at a maximum-security prison!" I accused. "We're going on vacation, amiga! Make room for a little fun in your life."

"There you go again," she said.

"What?"

"This isn't vacation, Harmony! When are you going to figure that out?"

"Probably about the same time you figure out you're being a big fat jerk. I can't believe you're making me toss everything I packed."

She pointed at the disco ball lamp. "I didn't make you get rid of that thing, did I?"

"*That thing?* I thought you liked it!"

"Sure, it's way fab. If you overlook that it's taking up valuable space and using who knows how many watts of our limited electricity," she retorted.

Lamont brought in Mello's second box. "So the big tour is off to a great start, huh?"

We finally got everything — or at least everything Trin allowed to stay — neatly put away in all the drawers, cabinets, and closets. When we finished, I had to admit (as much as I hated to) that Trin was right. Old Bessie was stuffed. And, of course, Sandie would add her things in the morning.

Still, I promised Mello I'd sneak in her shampoo ... and maybe the chocolate fountain. "How?" she asked.

"I don't know, Mello, but it must be done. When Trin goes psycho like this, we've got to band together to survive."

She gave me a quick hug. "Thanks, Harmony. You don't know what this means to me."

We were all discussing what time to pull out when my phone rang my mamma's tune.

I wandered away from Mello and answered.

"Harmony, Aunt Berta just called," Mamma said. "She finally worked out the details. She's gotten Lucinda a flight to San Francisco."

My heart began to pound. "I thought she'd given up on that idea," I whispered. "Mamma, we're leaving in the morning!"

"But you told me you wanted Lucinda to join you on the tour," Mamma said. "Don't tell me you've changed your mind!"

I sighed. "No, of course not. It will be a blast to see her."

I punched End and turned around to go back to the RV, trying to figure out the best way to tell Trin, who had just vetoed a three-point-five-ounce bottle of shampoo, that I planned to bring my cousin (and all her belongings) aboard for most of the tour.

I decided it might go better after I shared my next big surprise. I ran around getting everything in place and then called them out of the RV. "Walk straight toward me and don't turn around until I tell you to," I told them. When I gave the okay, they turned toward the RV and went totally crazy.

"It's us!" Trin screamed. "It's our picture on the side of the RV!"

"We're huge!" Mello added. "And we look so . . . cool."

Trin threw her hands up. "Well, yeah. What would you expect?"

Lamont crossed his arms. "It's OK that I'm not in the picture. Really. I'm not hurt. I mean, no one expects the soundman's picture to be posted on the—"

I grabbed his arm and took him back to the truck. The sign I'd stuck on the side had a picture of Lamont with the Chosen Girls logo and the words "Sound by Lamont" underneath.

"Well," he muttered. A slow grin spread across his face as he turned to me. "Well, that's all right, Harmony. Thanks."

"You're welcome," I answered. And then my heart started pounding as I got ready to break the news about Lucinda. *I'm only afraid because the RV is so crowded*, I told myself. *I'm not really worried about my cousin. I know Lucinda — surely she's not really doing bad stuff.*

Maybe I shouldn't have been so quick to say yes. But how could I tell my favorite cousin no? Anyway, it's too late now.

I took a deep breath and smiled at them. "And now, I have one last surprise to tell all of you about. Remember I mentioned my cousin Lucinda?"

chapter • 5

...

Thursday Morning

I watched the clock on my phone and declared, "The bell for first period is ringing … right … now!"

"Don't remind me," Mello moaned.

"Don't remind you of what?" I asked. "That instead of listening to a boring lecture on Romans and Greeks, you're —"

"Mr. Fargo's lectures are not boring, Harmony. And I think Roman history is —"

"Fascinating, I'm sure," I finished for her. "But why dwell in the past? *Today* is our day! We're living the dream, amigas! We are cruising the super slab in our deluxe fun-mobile."

"You know it!" Trin agreed, stretching her long arms and breathing deeply. "Should I pop in a DVD? I brought some great movies."

I looked out the window. "I'd rather watch all the people watching *us*. See them staring? Everyone's freaking out about passing a rock band on tour. Oh, I only love this."

"It's the huge signs you ordered. They're getting major attention," Trin agreed, waving at some gawking kids in the backseat of a minivan.

Mello reached for her book bag. "Well, we should probably go ahead and get our schoolwork over with."

"Mello, we've been on the road, like, fifteen minutes," I said, not even trying to hide my disgust. "We've got a week and a half to get the work done."

She put a folder on the table and pulled out a worksheet. "But if we get it done now, we'll enjoy the rest of the trip so much more."

I looked at Trin, who was eyeing her own book bag. "Trin!"

"Maybe she's right, Harmony. If we get it done now—"

"Come on, Trin! Don't let me down," I begged. "Where's your spirit of adventure? It's our very first morning of our very first U.S. tour."

Trin bit her lip. "Yeah, this is a pretty big deal," she said. "Put your stuff away, Mello. You're making me feel guilty."

"You *should* feel guilty. Both of you should. You said we'd help each other with schoolwork, Harmony. You promised. And I need help on this first question." Mello tapped her paper.

"Here, let me see it," I said.

She handed it to me. "It's number one. Who was the emperor of—"

I grabbed her folder off the table and shoved the paper back inside it. "I promised to help, but I didn't promise we'd finish before we drove out of Hopetown!"

"Harmony! Give my stuff back."

Trin reached for Mello's book bag and held it open for me. "In you go, vile homework!" she declared as I stuffed the folder inside.

"Trin!"

"We're just saving you from yourself, Mello," I explained. "We're doing this because we love you."

"I'm sure Mr. Fargo will accept that explanation when I tell him why I didn't finish the sheet," Mello said.

I smiled at her. "Relax. Think of all the times in your life I've talked you into something fun. Have you ever regretted … wait. On second thought, don't answer that. But you won't regret goofing with us today. For reals."

"Let's talk about the San Francisco concert," Trin suggested. "We've got to get ready for it, anyway, so that's not wasting time."

Mello wavered. "Well, maybe."

"I can't believe Candlestick Park is already sold out," I said. "Eleven thousand people! I can't wait to rock where the Beatles performed."

"And the Mug Shots," Mello added.

Trin smiled. "Ohwow, we're going to perform where the Mug Shots performed?"

"Cool frijoles, huh?"

"Yeah. But you know what's really cool?" she asked. "I mean, I like the Mug Shots. Their music is fun and all. But it's way cool that what *we* sing about *matters*. I mean, I want the people who come to totally rock out and have a blast—"

"Definitely," Mello agreed.

"But I'm glad that's not all there is to it, you know? Our message can bring people closer to God. We can make a forever difference in their lives," Trin finished.

I nodded. "Without that, this would all be pretty shallow, wouldn't it? It's cool being girls who rock for God."

"Ohwow! Song title alert," Trin exclaimed. "You with me on this, Mello?"

Mello started digging in her book bag.

I grabbed her hand. "No, Mello! No homework."

"I'm getting paper, Harmony. To write some lyrics."

I let go. "Oh. Right. Sorry."

"We need a new song for the tour, anyway," Trin said. "Let's call it 'Girls Who Rock for God,' and let's make it about why we do what we do."

I thought about that. "Because we can't hold it down. It's the right thing, you know? The real thing."

"First two lines!" Mello squealed. "Keep it coming, Harmony."

I shrugged. "Um ... I don't know. Help me out, Trin."

"When we sing, we're talking about what really matters in our lives," she answered. "It all comes down to Jesus, you know? He's the one who died for us."

Mello stared at her paper and drummed with her left hand. Then she started writing frantically, then scratching out words, and then writing more. Finally, she looked up and smiled. "How's this?"

Can't hold it down.
What we're about is
What we're all about.

The right thing.
The real thing.
Talking about what really matters
In our lives
In our dreams
And who lived for us
Who cried for us
Who died for us.

She turned a deep shade of red. "I mean, it still needs some work, of course. But—"

"I only love it!" Trin yelled, clapping her hands. "You're so good, Mello."

I nodded. "You are. It sounds great."

"Really?" Mello asked shyly. "Thanks."

Trin propped her elbows on the table. "You know what's sad? That so many people don't get it. They live their whole lives just, you know, lost."

Mello nodded. "Yeah. And half the time they're offended by the idea of Jesus. The very thing they most need to hear."

I thought about Lucinda. *Was she one of those people?* As Trin and Mello talked about faith in God, I began to wonder what we would sound like to my cousin. If she expected a typical rock band scene, she would get a pretty big surprise. Here we sat, quietly discussing all these deep life issues. We didn't even have the stereo on! She'd probably think we were the most boring excuse for a band ever.

As I looked at myself and my best friends from this new point of view, I started getting paranoid. I didn't feel as excited about being the "girls who rock for God." Part of me wished we could just be a normal rock band, who sang about stupid stuff that didn't matter. Stuff that wouldn't offend my cousin. Stuff that would make her think I was cool.

Maybe once Lucinda hooked up with us I could tone the "God stuff" down. Just a little. I didn't want to abandon my faith or anything, I just wanted to be sensitive to her needs.

I forgot about all that as we pulled into our RV park. The place was mostly pavement, but the parts that weren't were covered with brilliant green grass, red and yellow flowers, and orderly rows of palm trees.

I couldn't contain my excitement as we pulled into the parking lot and Sandie and Bob went to get our lot numbers. "Look at the cute clubhouse!"

"Harmony, it's just a two-story building covered with gray siding," Mello said.

"And bright white trim," I corrected. "And it's not just a building. It's the clubhouse at the scene of our first night on tour. The place where our adventure begins. Let's see if there's a little store inside. And maybe a workout room."

"We are not working out," Mello declared.

"That's the spirit!" I agreed. "We're on vacation."

There was a store inside. Mello found the canned goods aisle. "Look, Trin, if we need any other ingredients for dinner, they've got us covered."

Trin joined her. "If each of you brought everything on the grocery list I handed out, we're all good." She picked up a can. "Bet you're glad. They want a dollar fifty for this corn!"

"Uh, still, it's nice to know it's here," I said. "I mean, you know, if somehow we needed something."

Lamont elbowed me and whispered, "Harmony, did you forget your groceries?"

"Why didn't you remind me when we moved our stuff in? I still could have gone and—"

"Wait a minute," he interrupted. "You didn't forget. You handed me a box marked 'groceries,' remember? Trin put it under the sink because the cupboards were full."

I swallowed. "Oh, did that box say 'groceries'? Sí. Now I remember." He looked at me with a puzzled frown.

I tried to smile. The last thing I wanted Lamont—or anyone—to know right now was that I'd stashed a few no-no's in that box.

Our lot—or pad site—had a small patch of lawn with a picnic table on it. Lamont and Bob parked in the site next to us.

I had my hand on the doorknob, ready to head out and explore, when Trin yelled, "OK, everybody, man your posts."

"What posts?"

She rolled her eyes. "The 'setting up camp' posts. Look at the list on the cupboard door if you can't remember what you're supposed to do."

I found the list—a series of columns and rows with our names across the top and Day One, Day Two, etc., down the side. "Wow, this is pretty complicated," I commented. "Is this some kind of secret code?"

Mello laughed. "Harmony, you were with us when we made the chart! Remember? At Mr. and Mrs. C's house? Here, I'll help you."

Turned out I didn't need to leave the RV to find adventure. Popping the sides out, hooking up to electricity, and lowering the awning all fascinated me. Trin, Lamont, and Mello laughed at me the whole time, because I didn't have a clue what I was doing.

"Did you hear a single word Mr. C told us?" Trin asked.

"I think maybe I was a little distracted," I admitted. "I was planning how to decorate Old Bessie."

I guess it's a good thing Trin took the whole organization concept way seriously, because I found the menu posted on another cupboard door. It read "Night One: quesadillas, chips, and salsa," and listed ingredients with letters out to the side:

Chips — H

Salsa — L

Tortillas — M

Cheese — T

Another secret code. But I could figure this one out. H had to stand for Harmony. So I should have packed chips. I jogged over to the little store and got a bag for — ouch! — six dollars.

"This is the best food I've tasted. Ever," I announced as we ate at the outdoor picnic table.

Trin spooned more salsa onto her plate. "It did turn out all right, didn't it? Thanks, everybody, for bringing the groceries. See? If anyone had forgotten their ingredient, the meal wouldn't have been complete."

Whew. Good thing the store had those chips.

"Kinda like our band," Mello said, looking around at each of us. "If Harmony didn't play bass or Trin didn't sing—"

I smiled. "Or if we didn't have Mello on drums—"

"Or Lamont on sound," Trin added.

Mello nodded. "Without each of us, it just wouldn't be the Chosen Girls."

"See?" I asked. "I told you this trip was what we needed. The tour is already teaching us more about working together."

Sandie started crying. "This is just beautiful!" she said through sobs before she ran to the RV for a tissue.

I looked at Bob, and I was almost sure I caught the faintest trace of a smile.

Snuggling into my table-turned-bed that night, I couldn't stop smiling myself. What a great first day! And tomorrow — San Francisco. And Lucinda!

"Good night, girls," Sandie said as she laid the huge passenger seat back into a bed.

"Good night, Sandie," we called back to her.

"Harmony, you were brilliant to think of traveling in an RV," Mello said as she slipped into bed beside me.

"No doubt!" Trin called from her diva room. "This is the best trip of all time. You get the genius award for the year, Harmony."

"Yeah, well. We haven't done anything yet. It will only get better from here," I promised.

chapter • 6

. . .

Someone whispered in my ear. "Harmony! Psst—Harmony!"

"What?" I asked, trying to pull out of the deep sleep I was enjoying.

"Shh! Don't wake up Trin."

I opened my eyes and saw, in the darkness, Mello's face just a few inches from my own. "You're awake before me?" I asked as I looked around the RV. "Before anyone . . . before daylight, even. What's going on?"

"Where'd you put the shampoo?"

"Shampoo?"

I felt her breath as she huffed in frustration. "My contraband bottle. You promised to sneak it on board. Remember?"

"Oh. Right."

"Tell me quick. I want to take my shower before Trin gets up and figures out I'm not using Latherē."

I propped myself up on one elbow. "You're not messing around about this shampoo deal, are you? This has got to be the first time you woke up without me having to—"

"Get me the shampoo!"

I took a deep breath as I considered how to break the news. "I might have forgotten the shampoo, Mello."

"What?"

"I don't know for sure. Things got so crazy right before we left, and I—"

"Did you bring the chocolate fountain?"

"You know it! And the sparkling—um, I mean, I think I got the fountain."

"But you forgot my shampoo?"

I sat up and swung my feet to the side of the bed. "Let me check the box. Maybe I put it in there."

She hovered over me as I pulled the box marked "groceries" out of the lower cabinet. I slowly pulled the tape off the top.

"Faster!" Mello demanded.

"I don't want to wake up Trin. I'm trying to be quiet," I explained. But I also wasn't in any kind of hurry, because I really didn't think the shampoo would be in there. At least, I didn't remember putting it in. Still, I clung to the hope that somehow it might have found its way—

"No shampoo!" Mello hissed as she dug through the box. "Harmony, you brought the fountain, the cider, *and* the stemware, but you couldn't put in my one measly bottle of—"

I didn't want to hear it. "Exactly, Mello. One measly bottle of shampoo. Listen to yourself! Why don't you quit being such a shampoo snob and lower yourself, for just a few days, to using my brand?"

She slammed the box down and the glasses clinked together. "Oh! You so do not get this!"

"And you so better not break my stemware, or—"

"Stemware?"

Mello and I froze as Trin's questioning voice broke into our argument. Trin stomped over to the box and looked inside. "Stemware. And the cider and the chocolate fountain."

Mello shoved the box farther away from herself. "All Harmony's idea."

I felt the heat rising to my face. "Mello, you know you wanted me to—"

"To bring shampoo. I admit it. I asked you to bring my tiny bottle of shampoo, which is a matter of hygiene, thank you very—"

I crossed my arms. "Like hygiene is more important than having a good time."

"I hope sleeping on a chocolate fountain with stemware for your pillow is your idea of a good time, Harmony," Trin said. "Because once your cousin moves in, there's not gonna be anywhere else for this stuff to go."

"Hey," I argued. "You said you wanted Lucinda to come—that you thought it would be fun."

Trin sighed. "Yeah, Harmony, but it's going to mean some sacrifices for all of us. You don't get that, do you? There's only so much room in here. When Lucinda comes, she's not bringing more space with her. We'll each give up some space. See? When you choose one thing, it means you're not choosing something else. You can't have it all."

I closed the box and shoved it back under the cupboard. Then I stood up and announced, "Well, I, for one, intend to try."

Trin and Mello, on the other hand, seemed determined that I fail. Starting with my shower.

Someone banged on the door. "Harmony, get out, now!" Trin yelled. "You've probably already used all the hot water, and there are two of us waiting."

I squirted Latheré in my hand. "I just got in!"

"Ten minutes ago. Hurry up!"

I took my time working up a good, sudsy lather, thankful Sandie had taken her shower the night before. At least she wasn't hounding me.

Maybe two minutes later Mello called, "Harmony, are you almost finished?"

"I'm rinsing my hair. Why didn't you take your shower last night?"

"Why didn't you take *your* shower last night?"

I soaped my legs. "I like to start the day with a shower. It's invigorating."

"Tomorrow you can go last," she said. "It'll be plenty invigorating, I bet. Like, forty degrees cold invigorating."

Their harassment didn't end with the shower. Trin tried to push me away from the mirror. "Harmony, scoot over. I need to see too."

"But I got here first."

"Yeah, well. If you're gonna hog the whole thing, at least make it quick."

I rolled my eyes. "This coming from the diva who takes forty-five minutes to apply *clear* lip gloss."

"I don't like it outside my lip line, OK? Ew."

"Harmony, can't you free up one plug?" Mello asked. "I need to plug in my blow-dryer."

"You could let your hair dry naturally," I suggested.

She pouted. "Did I say it's for my hair? I planned to use it on my fingers and toes. I know I have frostbite after taking that shower."

Trin looked at the electrical outlet. "Yeah, Harmony, why do you need a curling iron *and* a straightener?"

"Because I'm doing the back of my hair straight, but I'm gonna do two little curls right here," I answered, holding up two small sections of my black hair. "There's a plug in your room, Trin."

Mello marched past me to the bedroom. A second later the lights went out and everything electric made a loud *beep*.

"Way to go, Mello," I yelled. "You blew a fuse."

She came back in and glared at me. "Oh, no, Harmony. That was nothing compared to the fuse I'm gonna—"

Trin stepped between us. "Harmony, go flip the switch and turn the power back on."

"I don't see why I should have to—"

"Now."

"Fine." I stood up and looked around.

Trin shook her head. "You don't know where the fuse box is, do you?"

I shrugged.

"You are worse than useless," said Trin.

"What happened to brilliant?" I asked. "Last night you called me genius of the year."

"Sorry, the members of the committee changed their minds," she answered as she led me to the fuses.

I ran into Lamont later when I stepped outside to get some fresh air and a little space. "You are so lucky you're not in there with—," I began.

"Oh, no," he countered. "Don't talk to me about lucky. Could you hear Bob snoring?"

I giggled. "Lamont, I'm in the RV."

He looked around and leaned closer to me. "Harmony, I would have guessed people back in Hopetown could hear the man. The walls of that pop-up were moving in and out like in the old Mickey Mouse cartoons." He gave a realistic-sounding impression of a deep, rumbling snore. "I didn't sleep a bit. I'm gonna crash from here to San Francisco today, though, so don't call every five minutes like you did yesterday."

"But who'll chat it up with Bob if you're asleep?" I asked.

Lamont said, "I'd be worried about that, but I'm pretty sure he unloaded all his deep, dark secrets yesterday. There's really nothing left between us that needs to be said."

"Are you serious?" Now I looked around, then leaned in closer. "What did he say?"

"He said, 'Always wanted to drive up the coast.'"

"And?"

"That was it."

"Lamont, we were on the road for *hours* and *hours* yesterday. That's all he said?"

He shrugged. "I think he was too busy listening to his country music."

"Oh, Lamont!" I cried. "*Country?* I'm so very sorry!"

"Anything for the Chosen Girls," he answered with a grin.

I figured attitudes would improve once we got on the road.

I figured wrong.

For one thing, driving didn't seem quite as exciting, even though people still pointed at us and waved. And it didn't take long for the thrill of watching movies to wear off.

After a while, Mello dug a quilt out of one of the cup-boards. "Isn't it amazing?" she asked. "It's my mother's prized possession. My great-grandmother made it, and my mom's all sad because some of the patches are threadbare. I snuck it out of the house, and I'm going to restore it as a birthday surprise for her." She spread out tiny squares of fabric on the table. "See? I ordered these from a website that re-creates vintage fabrics."

Trin leaned closer. "Ohwow! That is so thoughtful, Mello! Your mom is so going to freak."

I glanced through the bead curtain at the driver's seat and wasn't surprised to see Sandie reach for a tissue.

Trin got out her scrapbook stuff. "I'm going to make a scrapbook of our tour, so we can remember this trip forever."

I looked for my jewelry-making stuff. "It's not here," I said after I searched through the cabinets. "I can't believe it! I guess I forgot my beads and wire."

Mello looked thoughtful. "You forgot something *you* wanted to bring? Wow, that is a surprise."

I rolled my eyes. "You're still not over the shampoo issue? Your hair looks—ew! I was about to say 'your hair looks fine,' but Mello, it looks like you shampooed with vegetable oil!"

She threw her hands in the air. "Oh! Thanks, Harmony, for finally recognizing what I tried to tell you back in—"

Trin took a closer look at Mello. "Gross! It's all clumped together in strings. There is no way you even used the Latherē. Did you just not wash it to make a point?"

"No," Mello answered. "I washed it with Latherē. And while I appreciate the fact that you both believe me now, I think I've heard enough negative comments about my hair. It's not my fault it looks like this."

Trin nodded. "Gotcha. Sorry, Mello. We are *so* going straight for shampoo first thing in San Francisco. Any kind you want."

I whispered, "Let's pick up some earplugs for Lamont while we're at it."

• • •

We finally reached San Francisco and pulled into the parking lot of the venue where we'd perform that night. We stepped down from the RV and stared up at the walls of Candlestick Park.

"Ohwow, how cool is this?" Trin asked. "And what a relief to be here hours ahead of time. We can go in, set up, and run a sound check without worrying about—"

"Wrong!" I interrupted. "We got here early so we could see the city. We're within walking distance of Chinatown and Fisherman's Wharf—two of San Francisco's major attractions. Which one do you want to see first?"

"Harmony," Mello whined. "I'd feel better if we just set up and—"

I raised my eyebrows. "Do you want new shampoo before tonight's concert? Fisherman's Wharf is a major shopping destination."

Mello ran her hands through her nasty hair. "Shampoo? Definitely. OK, I'm in."

Lamont strode up and immediately offered his opinion. "Not smart, women. You do not need to be taking off right before the biggest concert of—"

I pouted. "Too bad. I so wanted to buy you some earplugs so you could sleep tonight."

He started tapping his foot. "Earplugs?"

"Really good ones too. But maybe tonight won't be as—"

"OK, go. But get back here in three hours."

"You aren't coming, Lamont?" Trin asked.

He looked at the truck. "Right. I only have to unload all the equipment, find someone to help me run a sound check, and make sure the monitors coordinate with the—"

"Got it. We'll see you in a few hours!" I called as I headed for the wharf with Mello and Trin right behind me. "See? I printed out these maps before we left home. And one tells all about Fisherman's Wharf. Talk about an exciting place. Pier 39 is supposed to be like a carnival, and there's Fish Alley, where they keep all the fishing boats and ship museums, and—I saved the best for last—Ghirardelli Square!"

"Ghirardelli Square? You're just dragging us along on your search for some serious chocolate, aren't you?" Trin asked.

I tapped my paper. "It's actually referred to as a brick factory converted into a 'shopping mecca,' thank you very much. But since it's named after one of the most famous chocolate makers ever, I'm guessing they'll have chocolate somewhere."

Trin's smile grew. "Shopping mecca? It actually says that? Ohwow, let's walk faster."

The Internet article hadn't lied about Fisherman's Wharf. It took us a while to find our way, but once we got there—wow! It felt like a festival about to spill over the edge of the pier and into the water. Rides, vendors, restaurants, music, boats, and more people than I'd seen in one place in ages—not counting our concerts. The bright colors of umbrella tables and sounds of live bands totally energized me.

This looked like a place for adventures.

We found shampoo for Mello right off. Of course, we found some fun shower gel and lotion too. Trin seemed to have forgotten about her list and its limits, and Mello and I sure didn't remind her.

The earplugs were harder to find, but we finally found some for swimming that we hoped would at least help a little with the noise from Bob's snoring. And we ate freshly caught seafood at an amazing restaurant that overlooked the bay. Then we hit the fun shops.

Trin was trying on her thirteenth outfit when Mello's phone rang. She answered, listened, said "thanks," hung up, and screamed. "It's time! We're supposed to be back already. That was Lamont."

"Ohwow," Trin said, "we'll get moving. But I must have the pink sweater, the white T-shirt, and the jeans. Harmony, will you check out for me while I change?"

I gathered the clothes Trin had named and added a San Francisco sweatshirt I only loved to the pile. "Sí, but you'll have to let me get some chocolate before we head back. I saw the shop — it's across the hall."

Mello made a face. "Harmony! We don't have time."

"Here, then," I said, shoving the clothes into her arms. "You check out for Trin while I get chocolate. Bet I'll finish before you do."

Actually, we finished at the same time. We each had a couple of bags to carry as we threaded our way back through the shops and throngs of people to the street.

"Is this where we turn?" Trin asked at the third intersection.

Mello shrugged. "It looks familiar, but we made, like, forty turns on all these little streets. They all look alike to me. Harmony, check your map."

"Sure," I said, putting my bags on the sidewalk and reaching into my pocket.

Then my other pocket.

Then my back pockets.

Trin rolled her eyes. "Very funny, Harmony. But we don't have time for jokes. It's still a long walk from here. We're barely going to be able to brush our hair and tune before the concert."

"Oh, no. Brushing will not do it. I am *so* washing my hair before we walk onto that stage," Mello insisted.

Trin frowned at Mello's greasy mop of hair. "Agreed. So let's have the map."

By now I was digging through my shopping bags. "It's not here. For reals. I think I must have thrown it away somehow. Maybe at lunch."

"Harmony! We'll never find our way to the arena!" Trin yelled. "Do I need to remind you tonight's concert is sold out? Eleven thousand people will be there waiting to see us!"

Mello started crying. "I told you we shouldn't come, Harmony. We should have stayed at the arena and gotten ready. But no, you had to see the city. You had to have adventure."

Trin picked up her bags and stomped away from me. "I don't know where I'm going, but we can't just stand in one spot. I hope getting lost in downtown San Francisco right before a concert is enough adventure for you, Harmony, because it's the *last* adventure we'll have on this tour."

• • •

chapter 7

By the time I caught up to Trin, she was sobbing out our sad story to a store clerk who, unfortunately, didn't seem to speak English.

Or Spanish.

I stepped up to the counter and asked, "Taxi?"

He unleashed a string of words in whatever language he *did* speak, and then wrote out a phone number on a scrap of paper. I punched the number into my phone and smiled in triumph as the person on the other end answered, "Turbo Taxi service. How can I help you?"

"My friends and I need a taxi to Candlestick Park," I answered, trying my best to sound like I ordered taxis all the time.

"And where would you be now?"

I looked around the store and then admitted, "I don't know where we are."

"Then we're going to be unable to —"

Trin grabbed my elbow. "The street signs! Come on!"

"Wait," I begged as I ran to the corner. "We're at the inter-secton of, um, Oakwood and Willowwood. A few blocks from Fisherman's Wharf."

"We'll send someone right out. They should reach you in about twenty minutes."

"Twenty minutes?" I screeched.

"Do you want to cancel the taxi?"

I took a big breath. "No. No, twenty minutes will be fine."

I hung up and looked hopefully at Trin and Mello. "I know it's a long wait, but it took longer than that for us to walk here, and it'll probably only take the taxi a few minutes to —"

"Sounds good. I'm just going to pop back in that store while we wait," Trin said. "They had some serious earrings on the counter!"

Mello sat on the curb. "I'm actually glad we don't have to walk anymore. My feet are killing me, and the handles of these bags are *so* digging into my hands."

• • •

The taxi came in just ten minutes and took less than five getting us to the arena. We rushed into the RV, where Mello immediately began to shower and Trin and I started on our hair and makeup.

Trin growled at her reflection. "Look at my hair! This is not a good time for it to refuse to cooperate."

"What if you did this?" I asked, pulling her long pink mane into two low ponytails.

She screamed.

"OK, sorry," I said, dropping her hair.

"No! That was a happy scream! I love it. Do it again. Here, use these hair bands."

Mello emerged from her shower before I even finished my stage makeup. "Well, if nothing else, getting ready in ten minutes flat helps us remember it's not about how we look."

"Good thinking, Mello," Trin said. "But we better leave time to pray, because that *is* what we're all about."

"Let's pray in the arena," I suggested. "I want to look at the seats where people will be sitting, you know?"

Trin stood up. "I'm ready."

"Me too," Mello said.

Trin and I turned to look at Mello. Her cheeks were rosy, her lips were pink, and her eyes twinkled under a thin line of silver glitter. The front of her still-damp hair was pulled into a ponytail high on top of her head, and she had already sprayed on her blue highlights.

Trin shook her head. "I'll never understand how you do that."

"What?"

"Go totally glam in, like, two seconds."

Mello smiled. "When you're friends with someone as disorganized as Harmony, you learn to do a lot of stuff fast."

• • •

The arena took my breath away. Rows and rows of red folding chairs filled the floor area, and then the stands began. Lower, middle, and upper levels formed an egg-shaped ring all the way around the building, but the huge stage, standing at least ten feet high and stretching maybe thirty feet across, blocked off one end of the oval.

I almost fainted at the thought that tonight I'd be on that stage, and every seat in front of me would be filled. All at once I understood what Mello, Trin, and Lamont had been trying to tell me. This wasn't just another concert. This was a *very* big deal.

We made our way past security guards and onto the stage. Lamont met us there, shaking his head. "You women scared me half to death. I didn't think you'd make it. And now you come ambling in, all glammed up, like nothing even—"

"Sorry, Lamont," I said quickly. Then I pointed to our instruments, already out of the cases and plugged in. "But look at you! You are one amazing man. You've got us totally hooked up."

He struck a pose. "But of course." Then he laughed. "Jonah's sound and light guys ... Man, I'm learning so much from them on this tour. You are gonna freak when you see all the stuff they've got going on."

"So should we tune first or pray first?" Mello asked.

"I'm totally feeling the need to pray," I admitted.

Trin held her hands out to us. "Me too."

The four of us grabbed hands and made a circle on the stage. My heart beat faster as I bowed my head, and I felt that sense of awe I always have when I think about the privilege of talking to almighty God.

"Thanks, God, for giving us this opportunity," Trin began. "I am blown away to find myself onstage in this huge arena. Work through us tonight."

Mello went next. "Help me, God, to forget my fears. This isn't about me. It's about you and the people you want to reach in this place."

"God, you've blessed the Chosen Girls," Lamont prayed. "But you haven't blessed them so they can just sit back and enjoy the money and fame they're receiving. You've blessed them because you want them to be a blessing to people who need to know you, and people who need to know you better. Use them tonight to accomplish this, I pray."

I felt my eyes getting all watery, and I had to let go of Lamont's hand to wipe away the tear that started down my face. "God, this is amazing. I don't know why you've chosen us, but thank you. Help us do our best tonight—not so we'll look good, but so *you'll* look good. We want the glory to go to *you*."

We all said, "Amen." When we looked up, he was right beside us—Jonah Harrison!

"Mind if I join in?" he asked—and then stepped between Trin and I and took our hands! Before I could even say anything, he was praying. "Thanks, God, for bringing the Chosen Girls onboard for this tour. I can already sense the way you are working in them and through them. Be with them tonight. Be with me tonight. Use all of us, God, for we are yours. Amen."

After the prayer, we all shook hands with Jonah. I thought Lamont might pass out, he was so happy. Thankfully he didn't, because he had to get back to work.

After we tuned and ran through a couple of verses each from a few of our songs, an assistant took us backstage to wait.

We threaded through cement corridors that reminded me of tornado shelters or underground bunkers or something— not at all glamorous. Finally, we reached the room where we were supposed to hang out until they came to get us. It was just a big, plain room, but it had a few folding chairs and a table set up with some snacks and bottled water.

I pointed to the table. "Is that for us?"

The assistant smiled. "Sure is," she answered. "Sorry we didn't find out ahead of time what you like. Let me know—certain brands of crackers, chips, candy, whatever—and we'll have it waiting for you in Portland."

She stepped out, and we jumped up and down and squealed. "Whatever we want!" Trin said, grabbing the can of mixed nuts.

"How fun is this?" Mello asked, taking a bag of chips and settling into a chair.

I found a bag of M&Ms. "Cool frijoles. This, I could get used to."

Another assistant came in and handed us each a piece of paper. "Here's tonight's schedule. I know we've been over this via email, but I thought you might feel better if you got to look it over one last time before you go onstage. Any questions?"

We talked details for a few minutes, and I really did feel better. After she left, we got out our bags to spruce up. I was just applying my new sparkly lip gloss when the first assistant walked in and said, "Chosen Girls, it's time!"

My heart jumped into my throat, and I was so glad I didn't have to sing. We grabbed hands and walked side by side back through the corridors and into the darkened arena. I could hear the voice of an announcer saying, "They've taken the music world by storm—a fresh young band that is making a difference."

The assistant led us with her flashlight up a set of stairs that took us to the back of the stage. We walked around the backdrop and found our places just as the announcer said, "Help me welcome ... the Chosen Girls!"

The roar of the crowd—cool frijoles—blew me away. We've had loud audiences before, but never anything like this one.

We hit our first note, and the light show began. Lamont was right—it was amazing. Colored beams splashed across the stage, changing in time to the music. Fog rose in front of us and swirled in the lights, making designs in red, yellow, blue, and green. It was so pretty I almost forgot to play my bass.

Just for a minute, though. Then I remembered who I was and why I was onstage in the middle of all the action, and I totally came to life. Trin and I danced all over that massive stage, jamming like never before on our guitars. I felt sad for Mello, stuck behind her drums. Until I looked at her banging away and singing her heart out. She was anything but stuck behind her drums.

As we played, scenes from all our music videos flashed behind us on the massive screens. There we were, dressed as superheroes—twenty feet tall—as we battled the bad guys in the power of the Holy Spirit. I had to remind myself again to keep playing—I would have loved to sit and watch.

After we finished the set, we ran offstage while the crowd was still screaming and jumping up and down. Then Jonah went out, and the crowd got even louder!

An assistant set us up near a monitor so we could watch and listen. I kind of wondered how the massive crowd would make the transition from rock concert to special speaker, but I shouldn't have worried. Jonah held their attention—and ours—easily. It didn't hurt, I figured, that he's painfully good-looking. But he's also a compelling speaker—very funny at times, emotional at other times. And obviously, as Lamont liked to say, "tight with God."

We made our way quietly onstage as Jonah wrapped up his talk. He invited anyone who wanted to make a fresh commitment to God to come forward and stand at the base of the stage. We played a soft song as people began to come.

Tears poured down my face as I watched the area fill up until people had to stand in the aisles. Still, they came. Guys, girls, teenagers, adults—all praying, crying, reaching out to God. It was beautiful.

I thought about the ride up in the RV and how—for a while—I had wished our band could be a "normal rock band."

Still fingering my bass, I looked at the crowd in front of me. Those people giving themselves to God would never be the same because of tonight.

I promised myself I'd never again question the calling of the Chosen Girls.

• • •

After the service ended, we signed autographs and met hundreds of fans. Way cool. Then Trin, Mello, and I hopped into a taxi and headed for the airport to pick up Lucinda.

We met her at baggage claim. Any nervousness I felt about the "new and unimproved Lucinda" vanished as soon as I spotted her. She came running and threw herself at me, almost knocking me down. "Harmony! My famous rock-star cousin!"

I laughed and gave her a big hug.

"Lucinda, this is Mello and this is Trin," I said, pointing to my best friends.

She looked them over and smiled a brilliant smile. "I can tell you two are amazingly cool. We're going to have some serious fun together!"

Trin and Mello smiled back and, just like that, our little trio of friends became a quartet. Mis amigas didn't even complain when they saw Lucinda's enormous suitcase.

Oh, yeah, I thought. *Today's worries are behind us. Ahead, I see nothing but fun.*

chapter • 8

• • •

Lucinda woke us up the next morning by singing that old country song "On the Road Again" with a major twang. Even Mello laughed—and Mello is not usually one who likes to be awakened by anything other than a very gradual increase of sunlight. Or maybe the smell of cinnamon oatmeal.

"I know what you're thinking," Lucinda said to Trin when the song finally ended. "You're trying to figure out how to rewrite your songs so I can be onstage with you."

Trin looked panic-stricken.

Lucinda punched her on the arm. "Just kidding! I know I'm not a singer. Although, if I remember right, I'm way better than my cousin here."

"You got that—," Mello began. She caught my eye and said, "Um, wrong. I mean, not that you're even worse than Harmony. Oops! That didn't come out right, either."

I laughed. "It's OK, Mello. I've come to terms with the fact that I'll never sing for a living."

Mello threw a protective arm around me. "But you should hear her on bass," she told Lucinda.

Lucinda smiled. "I guess I will."

I clapped my hands. "I can't wait for you to hear us in concert."

"Me either," she agreed. "But for now—I'm guessing the hot water is a big issue in here. How do you decide who gets to shower first this morning?"

"Not Harmony," Trin and Mello said at the same time. Mello explained, "She went first yesterday."

"We need to schedule a rotation. See?" Trin asked, pointing to the charts. "We've got one for dishes and all the chores, but ... whoops! We didn't add you to the chore list."

Lucinda pretended to burst into tears. She sobbed and wiped her eyes and grabbed one of Sandie's tissues to do this huge, disgusting, fake blowing-of-her-nose thing. "I can't believe I don't get to participate in the chores! I'm just so hurt!"

Giggling, I said in my sweetest voice, "I'll share mine with you, Lucinda."

She turned off the tears so quickly we had to laugh. "What? Are you crazy? Like I'm gonna—" She stopped to look at the list. "Like I'm gonna flush your black water tank. I don't even know what a black water tank is."

"That's the tank that holds waste from the—"

Lucinda interrupted. "Correction! I meant to say, I don't *want* to know what it is. But back to the shower. I propose a dance-off to see who's first."

Mello cried, "A dance-off? Lucinda, it's not even nine in the morning. I can barely get myself out of bed, much less—"

"Looks like you're the loser, then, Miss Mello. Check this out." Lucinda cranked the RV's stereo to full blast and started busting major moves. Well, as major as you can get in a two-foot-square space.

I ran for the disco light and plugged it in.

"Wow!" Trin said. "You're seriously good, Lucinda. I don't even want to go up against—"

"No way," I argued. "Come on, Trin. You've taken dance since birth. Let's see what you've got."

Lucinda kept dancing. "Not yet! You've got to see my grand finale!" She dropped to the floor to do the Worm.

We rolled with laughter until we heard the *thunk* of her head hitting the bedroom door.

"Lucinda! Are you OK?" I asked.

"Somebody get me a paper towel," she answered. "I think I'll need it to stop the blood."

Mello jumped up and grabbed the roll, handing a few sheets to Lucinda. "Lucinda, I'm so sorry! Are you going to be all right?"

She wadded up the towels and held them to her head. "I don't know. I think, maybe, if I get in the shower . . ."

"Sure," Trin and Mello agreed.

She pulled the paper towels away and laughed. There was no blood. "Gotcha! But I'll be fast. I promise."

And she was. Trin had barely finished the new shower rotation chart by the time Lucinda got out.

"What's with all the charts?" Lucinda whispered once we were on the road. Trin and Mello were looking at magazines in the bedroom, so Lucinda and I had the living area to our-selves. "Your friends are obsessed."

"They're not obsessed. They're just ... organized," I countered.

"Oh, no. What they are goes way beyond organized. 'Harmony, don't forget to check the holding tank.' 'It's your turn to set the table.' 'Your T-shirt is on the floor.' 'Your right shoe is not perfectly aligned with the — '"

I shushed her. "OK! It's not like I haven't noticed. Sometimes I think they're worse than Mamma."

"Exactly," Lucinda agreed. "What's the point of taking off with your amigas if you have to spend the whole time clean-ing and following rules and junk?"

"That's what I think! This is the chance of a lifetime, you know? We should be chilling, not stressing. But I can't con-vince them."

Lucinda patted my arm. "And that, my dear cousin, is why Lucinda is here to save the day."

• • •

As we drove, I noticed that, besides the waving, smiling fans passing us on the road, there was some amazingly beautiful scenery. We stuck to Highway 101, driving straight up the coast. In places, the hills leading down to the Pacific were so picture-perfect I had to call everyone to look.

Soon after we crossed into Oregon, we drove into our RV park at Gold Beach, right where the Rogue River meets the ocean.

Even Trin jumped out of the RV before reminding us of our "setting up camp" chores. We stood together and turned in a slow circle, taking in the bright blue river against the deep green of the heavily forested hills. "Ohwow, I only love this place," Trin whispered.

"Just wait until our hike," I told her. Then I winked. "But not until after we set up camp."

"Right!" she said. Then she raised her voice. "Everybody, man your posts."

It was Lamont's turn to cook, and we were all pretty nervous. Mello insisted on putting out the leftover chips and salsa. "That way, even if the rest is a disaster, we'll have *something* to eat."

Lamont caught on right away. "What are the chips doing on the table? Chips are not on the menu tonight."

"We, um, thought they'd make a good appetizer," Mello said.

"Uh-huh. I know what you were really thinking. But you had no need to fear, for Chef Lamont is in the house. Check out this deluxe mac and cheese." He set a huge steaming pot in the middle of the picnic table.

We peeked inside. "It looks all right," Trin said.

"Smells good," Lucinda added.

I said, "Then let's quit talking about it and pray, so we can find out if it tastes good."

It did. But we didn't brag on Lamont too much, because he was too busy bragging on himself to listen.

After we ate, Trin stood up to gather plates. "Harmony's turn to wash dishes."

I frowned. "I'll wash them after our hike."

"No way," Mello argued. "That's against the rules. We can't go until the dishes are clean."

"But it's going to get dark soon," Lucinda complained.

I nodded. "Or it might start raining. It rains, like, all the time in Oregon."

Trin handed me the stack of plates. "Then you better hurry and get these washed."

I stomped into the RV and put the dishes on the counter. As I turned on the hot water, Lucinda came in. "Great!" I said. "Help me get these done so we can go hiking."

"This is stupid," she griped. "Why does it matter if you wash the dishes now or later?"

I added soap to the sink and started scrubbing the first plate. "It's part of our camp rules. We all agreed to the rules before we left."

She lay down on the couch. "I didn't agree to anybody's rules. I'm telling you, your friends are messed up."

I didn't answer.

Lucinda pointed out the window. "Look at this place. Forests, hills, a real-live river. All that land for exploring, and where are we? Stuck inside, scrubbing dishes."

I added another plate to the drain rack. "Actually, I don't see you scrubbing anything."

"Why didn't you just get paper plates?"

"Trin decided they take up too much space. And Mello doesn't like to waste trees."

"But she doesn't mind wasting time, huh? Time when she could be out there *hugging* trees?"

I attacked a blob of stuck-on cheese. "If you're in such a hurry, get your lazy self off the couch and come rinse, Lucinda."

"I'll do better than that. I'll take care of the last few plates," she offered.

I looked up in surprise. "Thanks!"

She started opening cupboard doors. "No problem. See? Just stick them up here, and we'll wash them when we get back."

"Lucinda!"

"What? You know it won't make any difference when they get washed, as long as they do get washed."

"But why not go ahead and—"

She tapped the window. "Because it's going to get dark! Look out there, Harmony. If we wait a minute more, they'll say it's too late to hike. We'll end up sitting around playing some dumb board game or something."

I looked at the open cupboard door. "Knowing Trin, she'd probably check in there."

Lucinda shrugged. "Then find your own spot. But let's *go*, girl. Now!"

I picked up the last few dirty plates and looked around the RV. "It's not like I'm not going to wash them," I explained, more to myself than Lucinda. "I mean, think of all that time on the road tomorrow with nothing to do. I could wash them then."

"Of course," she agreed.

I began to pull out one of the under-the-couch drawers when Lucinda whispered, "They're coming!"

I tipped the plates enough to stuff them in the drawer, slammed it shut, and jumped up. Turning around, I stuck both hands in the soapy sink water.

"Almost done?" Trin asked.

"Look," I answered. "No more dirty dishes on the counter."

Mello looked at me closely. "Don't get the water so hot next time, Harmony. Your face is flushed."

I pulled the sink plug. "Hot water kills more germs. So, everybody ready to hike?"

"Shouldn't we practice a little instead?" Trin asked. "We haven't finished our new song."

"No way. We need to work off that mac and cheese," I answered, poking Trin in the belly. "In San Francisco, I noticed your super suit is looking a little snug."

"Oh, really? Well, who ate three peanut butter cups today while we—"

"That's what I'm saying. We've done nothing but sit and eat all day. Let's get out there and—"

Mello interrupted us. "I don't know. I thought this might be a good night for a board game."

Lucinda coughed the word "loser" into her hand.

I put my arm around Mello. "Amiga, for someone who wants to protect the environment, you sure don't experience the environment much. Do you even know where we are?" I used a softer voice. "Don't you want to gaze upon that peacefully flowing river and hear the gentle wind whispering in the leaves? We'll probably never be here again. Ever."

She looked out the window. "Oh, OK. As long as it's more of a peaceful walk than an invigorating hike."

"Let's get Lamont," I said, opening the door.

Trin followed me out. "No, he said he wanted to take a nap."

"A *nap*?" Lucinda asked. She sounded offended.

Mello nodded. "Yeah. While Bob and Sandie are checking out the fishing. You know, before Bob starts snoring."

I shook my head. "So the earplugs didn't—"

"Apparently not."

• • •

We'd been on the trail only a few minutes when we ran into four guys headed back toward the park. The path wasn't wide enough for all of us, so we scooted to the edge to let them pass.

"Did you have a good hike?" Lucinda asked them.

A gorgeous blond answered. "Yeah. Nice place."

We nodded in agreement.

"Are you from around here?" another guy asked. He had spiked red hair and eyes as blue as the nearby river.

"Nah. We're from Hopetown. Near L.A.," I answered.

The tallest guy — he must have been six foot two — asked, "How long are you staying?"

Trin flashed her toothpaste-commercial smile at him. "Just tonight. We've got a concert in Portland tomorrow."

His face lit up. "You're the band! We saw your pictures on the RV."

Suddenly, all the guys came to life. "Oh, right."

"Dude."

"A band."

"Cool."

The blond ran a hand through his hair. "So, we're about to make a fire by the river. Roast some marshmallows ..."

The redhead punched him in the arm. "Dude. You make us sound so lame."

"It's not lame," I said. "I love bonfires. And roasted marshmallows."

Now Trin punched *me* in the arm. "Harmony," she whispered, "don't invite yourself!"

"So you wanna come?" Tall Boy asked, looking straight at Trin.

She shrugged. "We were just starting our hike."

Lucinda said, "I vote for the fire."

I didn't want Lucinda calling *me* a loser, so I smiled at the redhead. "Me too. We can hike any time."

Mello gave me this look that screamed, "What?!?!" and growled, "Back at the RV, you said we'd probably never be here again."

"But that doesn't mean we'll never hike again," I explained. "Just maybe not here."

Trin tugged me away from the boys and whispered, "Harmony, this isn't a good idea."

"Why?"

"We don't know them."

"Exactly," I agreed. "I'd like to *get* to know them."

She shook her head and whispered, "They don't seem like the kind of guys we need to be hanging around."

"Why?" I whispered back. "Because they're beyond good-looking?"

She rolled her eyes. "Something's not right. Look at the way they're dressed, for one thing."

"How shallow is that?"

"They seem kind of . . . rough. Please, let's just finish our hike."

I looked at Lucinda, chatting up the shortest guy. His black wavy hair was as glossy as her long straight hair. They looked cute together.

He started down the path we'd just walked up, and she followed him. "Come on, Chosen Girls," she called over her shoulder. "Let's roast some marshmallows."

The redhead looked at me, and I felt a moment of panic. What if Trin was right about the guys?

On the other hand, Trin was probably just being uptight again. And trying to make me uptight too. Lucinda sure didn't seem to have a problem going to the campfire. And if the guys *were* trouble ... well, hadn't I promised to look out for my cousin?

I nodded at the redhead, and he fell into step beside me as I followed Lucinda and the dark-haired guy.

"I'm not going to go," Trin said. "We need to get back, anyway. We've got a big day tomorrow."

"I'll go with you, Trin," Mello volunteered.

I looked back at them, standing together in the path. I tried to sound cool as I told them, "Whatever. It's your loss."

chapter • 9

• • •

Saturday Night

The guys actually knew what they were doing when it came to building a fire. They found a pit someone else had made, ringed with rocks and surrounded by logs big enough to serve as benches. It sat maybe twenty feet from the bank of the river.

As Lucinda and I helped gather sticks, the night seemed too perfect to be real. I loved the smell of the fire as it flickered and caught hold. The promise of warmth it offered made the chill in the air energizing. Beside us, the curving river reflected the hills and trees on the far bank. Diamonds sparkled in the reflection as the rays of the setting sun danced across the water.

It would have been an amazing night if it had only been me and my cousin. But throw in four handsome guys and ... well, I couldn't have been happier.

Tall Boy went to their campsite and came back with a package of marshmallows and some wire hangers. I breathed a sigh of relief. We really were going to roast marshmallows. Nothing to worry about.

But I was wrong.

It started with their language as we sat around the fire. The redhead threw out a string of nasty words in the middle of a story, like he thought I would be impressed. Hardly. His buddies followed suit until I wanted to cover my ears. Listening to their filthy language felt like being pelted with garbage—as if they were throwing rotten tomatoes and bruised bananas at me. Except I knew it would be easier to wash garbage off my face than it would be to clear their words from my brain.

I wanted to ask them to watch their mouths, but I knew that would make me look very uncool. I concentrated on my marshmallow and hoped they'd figure it out on their own.

They didn't. Instead, they started with jokes so rude my face burned—and not from the fire. The guys were so busy laughing at each other, they didn't notice I wasn't joining in.

Unfortunately, Lucinda *did* join in.

I figured she was just embarrassed and didn't know what to do, so I thought I'd make it easy on both of us. I stood up and handed my hanger to the redhead, who I knew by now was named Reede. "Thanks for the marshmallows. We've got to get back now, since we're hitting the road early tomorrow."

He grabbed my hand. "You can't go now, Harmony. The fun's about to begin."

I snatched my hand away, and Tall Boy laughed. "Yeah, we're gonna trash some campsites. Don't you want to help?"

"No, thanks," I answered. "Come on, Lucinda."

Lucinda rolled her eyes. "Don't be a baby, Harmony. Let's go with them."

I leaned close to her ear. "Are you serious? Do you even know how much trouble we could get in?"

"That's only if we get caught," she answered. "I never get caught."

I remembered what Mamma had said about Lucinda getting kicked out of school. "Never?" I asked.

She laughed. "OK, hardly ever."

So Mamma was right about Lucinda. Now I felt really nervous, but I made myself ask, "What's fun about ruining other people's stuff?"

"I don't know yet, but it's something to do. Something new."

I put my hand on her arm, as if my touch could change her mind. "Lucinda, I won't do this. And neither will you. Say good night, and let's go back to the RV."

The firelight flickered across her narrowed eyes. "You will not tell me what to do, Armonia Gomez."

"I will," I insisted. "I promised Mamma I would keep you out of trouble."

Lucinda's laughter usually reminded me of a bubbling brook. Now it sounded like the brook had begun to freeze, and huge chunks of ice replaced the tumbling water. "I'm surprised at you," she sneered, her mouth set in a straight, angry line. "You should know better than to make promises you can't keep."

I looked from her face to the faces of the guys around the fire. In an instant, the whole setting seemed transformed. Instead of a fun, innocent campfire, I felt like I had stumbled into something evil . . . and I wanted to escape.

But first I had to tell them all to stop. I knew—absolutely knew—what they planned to do was wrong.

But if my own cousin wouldn't listen to me, why would they? If I told them what I thought, I'd make a fool of myself. They'd all laugh at me, and call me names like Lucinda had. I hated being laughed at.

Besides, my one little voice wouldn't make any difference.

I hoped Mamma would understand why I had to leave Lucinda. I had promised to protect her, but Lucinda was right. That was a promise I couldn't keep.

"Be careful," I told her and turned to leave.

She grabbed my arm. "Where do you think you're going?"

"To the RV," I answered.

She smirked. "No way. You're not gonna run and tattle. You're staying with me until I say we're finished."

"Lucinda, I—"

She stood up next to me. "You're staying with me. And if you breathe so much as a word of this to anybody on your little 'Jesus tour'—ever—I'll tell them it was all your idea. Then you'll get a taste of what it's like to be in trouble. Real trouble."

The guys came up behind me, blocking any escape. Reede said, "That's right. Tell her, Lucinda." For a minute I thought they might try to hurt me, and I was scared out of my mind. But they just started herding us toward the RV campsites. I noticed each of them pick up a long, heavy stick as they walked.

Lucinda grabbed my arm, and I wiped away a tear as we followed along.

•••

As the early morning sun made its way through the slats of the RV's mini-blinds, I tossed and turned. I couldn't get comfortable in my bed ... maybe because my stomach hurt so much.

I opened my eyes the tiniest bit and saw Lucinda, sound asleep, next to me. Her long black hair spread out across her pillow, and her beautiful face looked like the face of an angel.

I breathed in and caught the scent of a campfire, and the events from the night before came rushing back to me.

My cousin was no angel.

I wanted to tell myself I'd just had a horrible nightmare — that the smashed chairs, the spray-painted graffiti, and the trash cans emptied on people's campsites were part of an awful dream. But the smell of smoke was real. I knew it had all happened ... and more. And I'd been there watching.

I wondered how many laws had been broken. I wondered if the police had been called yet.

No wonder my stomach hurt.

While I lay quietly, Lucinda stirred. When she opened her eyes she smiled at me. "Good morning, cousin!" she sang out in her regular, cheery voice.

"So how was the campfire?" Trin asked, poking her head out of the bedroom. "We didn't hear you come in last night."

"It was great. You should have come," Lucinda answered. "Those boys were so sweet. After we roasted marshmallows, we sat around and sang."

I looked at her in shock. How could she lie so ... completely? So easily?

Trin grinned. "That does sound fun. Well, I'm glad." She left and then popped back in. "Harmony?"

"Yes?"

"You didn't say anything. Did you have fun?"

Lucinda looked at me, hard.

"The fire was really nice," I managed. "It looked so pretty there by the river."

"Good. Well, I'm first in the shower today," Trin announced. "And I plan to take a long, hot one."

Lucinda laughed. "If you do, I'll reroute your microphone at tonight's concert. Everyone will *see* you, but they'll *hear* me."

Trin screamed. "Forget it! I'll be fast!"

Someone knocked on the door of the RV, and I almost jumped out of my skin. Was it the police? Mamma would be sad to know that I felt afraid of the people hired to protect me. I'd been raised to respect them, sure, but not to fear them.

Lucinda wrapped a blanket around her shoulders and opened the door.

It was Bob. "Sunday service out here in thirty minutes. Bring your cereal."

"Was that really Bob?" a sleepy Mello asked after we shut the door. She shuffled in from the bedroom and sat on the edge of the bed I'd been sharing with Lucinda. "That's got to be a record. Has he ever said that many words in a row?"

I couldn't even laugh.

• • •

We sat outside at the picnic table listening to Bob's short Bible study. He did a surprisingly good job, but I couldn't really concentrate. I just wanted to load up and hit the road, putting as much distance between me and the campground as we could. I felt like I was on high alert, expecting the authorities to come around the corner any minute.

To distract myself, I used my spoon to poke my crunchy peanut butter cereal balls down into the milk. Then I'd move the spoon and watch them pop back up. Kind of like my bad memories from the night before—no matter how hard I tried to push them down, they came popping up again.

Just when I thought Bob might wrap it up, a man in khaki shorts and a Hawaiian shirt walked up our table. "Sorry to disturb you," he said. "Just wondered if any of your property got damaged last night."

My heart began to hammer inside my chest.

Bob looked around. "Why d'ya ask?"

"Some hooligans on the grounds last night. Did plenty of damage. Had a couple of busted-up deck chairs myself, and my neighbor had some foul language painted on his RV."

I glanced at Bob. His face turned beet red. "Catch 'em?"

"Not yet, but I think we will," the man answered. "The police have been called. They're on the way."

I could hardly breathe.

Bob nodded. "Hope they get 'em. Make 'em pay."

Lucinda batted her long dark lashes at Bob, all sweetness and innocence. "I can't believe it. How could someone do such a terrible thing?"

I wanted to throw up.

Bob shook his head.

"Looks like your site got skipped, at least," the visitor offered. "I'm going to check with the rest of our neighbors."

"I don't get it," Trin said after he left. "What's fun about destroying people's stuff?"

Mello nodded. "Yeah. Creating, I can see. Making some-thing beautiful for people to enjoy, like a quilt ..." She looked at me. "Or a necklace. But destroying? Who does that help?"

"People who vandalize aren't thinking about helping, Mello," Lamont said. "They're messed up, so they want everything around them to be messed up too."

"Maybe we could help some of the people whose sites got damaged," Trin suggested.

"No!" I said, too loudly. Everyone turned to look at me. "Sorry. It's just that—" *I can't be at the scene of the crime when the police come! But I can't say that.* I thought hard. "Um, we've got a concert in Portland tonight, and I know you don't want to cut it close again."

Mello said, "Yeah, she's right. But it was a good idea, Trin."

• • •

When we pulled out of camp before the police arrived, I breathed a big sigh of relief.

Until Mello pulled out the under-the-couch drawer. "Ew! Who stuffed dirty dishes in here? Nasty!" She held them out for us to see.

Crud! Last night had been so awful, I'd forgotten all about the dishes.

Trin took them from Mello and stared me down. "Harmony, these have macaroni and cheese on them. And salsa."

I nodded, slowly. "I meant to wash them right after the—"

"Oh, no!" Mello screamed, leaning over to look in the drawer again. "Look at the quilt!"

She pulled it out, and I felt my stomach flip-flop when I saw the bright yellow and red blotches on the faded fabric.

Tears poured down Mello's face as she turned to me. "Why did you do this, Harmony? Why'd you put macaroni and cheese on my mother's favorite quilt?"

"I didn't know the quilt was in there!" I said. "I thought you kept it in the cabinet in the bedroom."

"But why did you put dirty dishes in the drawer?" she asked.

I wanted her to understand me, to believe me. "I didn't mean to ruin anything. I just wanted to hike. I thought I could wash the dishes after we got back."

"But you didn't even hike," she reminded me. "Because you met those boys. So you ruined something my great-grandmother made for no—"

"I'll fix it," I promised. "Give it to me. I'll get the stains out."

• • •

It wasn't as easy as I had hoped. The material was so fragile it tore if I scrubbed too hard. I ended up using a sopping wet rag and gently, slowly soaking each small section.

"If you had worked half this hard on the dishes, the quilt never would have gotten ruined," Trin pointed out. "Why don't you think about the choices you make, Harmony? Haven't you heard that actions have consequences?"

Before I got to answer, Mello started in. "I *so* can't believe you did that, Harmony. It's not like I can just buy a new quilt. It's an heirloom. Irreplaceable." She sniffed, patting her tear-filled eyes with one of Sandie's tissues. "Don't you have any respect for other people's property?"

Their words hurt—not just because of the quilt. I couldn't help applying their lectures to other choices I had made the night before, and I felt sick about it.

But I could hear it in their voices and see it in their faces—no amount of apologizing would make any difference now. I didn't try to defend myself. I just kept scrubbing, hoping I could make at least this one thing right.

The yellow spots faded to lighter, cream-colored stains, and the red blotches turned a pinkish orange. After that, no matter how hard I tried, nothing happened. It was the best I could do, and I knew in my heart it wasn't good enough.

Trin was right—my bad decision had major consequences. I hated that I had damaged something so precious to Mello. Not just the quilt, either.

It looked like my selfishness had damaged our friendship, and I wondered if that might be even harder to repair than the antique quilt.

My hands trembled as I held the ruined quilt out to her. "Mello, I—"

Before I could say more, she took the quilt from me and went into the bedroom. Trin shot me a nasty look, followed Mello, and shut the door behind them.

I was ready to share the blame with someone. I turned on Lucinda. "And how is it that you could lie your head off all morning?" I whispered. "Don't you feel guilty *at all* about last night?"

"You've got a lot of learning to do," she answered. "How you act right after you break a rule is crucial. And you are pathetic, cousin. Blushing, looking down, not eating your breakfast—a complete idiot could guess you did something bad."

"Because I did!" I blurted. "I'm so sorry, Lucinda, but I have a conscience! I can't watch all that go on and not feel sick about it."

"As long as feeling sick is as far as it goes," she said. "Because, remember, you will *not* tell a soul. Not unless you want your next press release to have 'Christian Rock Star Vandalizes RV Park' as its title."

chapter • 10

...

Sunday Night

Backstage in Portland that night, just before we went on, Trin laid out her super suit. "We're switching into these after the third song, right?" she asked.

"Right," I agreed. "Hey, is that something on your jacket?"

Trin turned the white top over, revealing a brown spot. She held it to her nose. "Harmony!"

"What?" I asked. "Why is everything my fault?"

"It's a peanut butter cup! You've been eating them nonstop this whole—"

"But I didn't get it on your ... oh, wait. Unless that extra one I left on the counter—"

"And *why* did you leave it on the counter? What am I supposed to do now?" she wailed. "I can't stand this anymore, Harmony! It's like you're a three-year-old!"

"Will this help?" a backstage assistant asked. "It's one of those laundry wipes for spots."

Trin hugged the woman. "Thank you! Yes, it should help."

She scrubbed frantically, and the spot came out just as another assistant called, "Chosen Girls, you're on."

Our show went great again, with another great crowd. During the last song, while people were coming forward, I couldn't stop crying. Just like last time, except this time I was crying for my cousin. I thought about how much I wanted Lucinda to give herself to God. Now I knew, for sure, that was what she needed.

But who was I to tell her that? I'd gone along with her and the guys. If anyone was having any influence here, she seemed to be the one influencing me.

For the worse.

• • •

The next morning we had a radio interview at a major Portland station. I sat there spewing out my perfect answers, smiling at fans through the huge glass window, feeling like the biggest hypocrite in the world.

Mello wanted to go to an art museum after the interview. No longer in the mood to be the big party planner, I just nodded and followed along. It was actually pretty cool — for an art museum.

Then, at last, we were back on the road. Before we left, of course, Trin had to give us the rundown of who had what chores for the day. As if we all didn't know the charts by now! Still, I knew better than to cause problems at this point, so I sat and listened obediently. I even ignored Lucinda, who sat behind Trin mimicking every move.

"So what are we doing today?" Mello asked once we'd finished our morning jobs. "I'm not in the mood to work on my quilt."

I sighed. "Mello, I said I'm—"

"It wasn't a slam on you, Harmony," she said. "I'm just not in the mood."

I reached for the box of DVDs. "Let's watch *A Girl Named Sanita*," I suggested.

"That sappy tearjerker?" Trin asked. "It always makes me cry."

Mello said, "No doubt. I've seen it, like, thirty times, and I still cry every time at the part where—"

"Where that old man dies?" Lucinda asked.

"Yeah."

"Me too," Lucinda admitted. "What's your deal, Harmony? I thought you called this the fun-mobile. You trying to turn it into a sap-mobile instead?"

I shrugged. I had wanted to watch sad movies so I could cry without being obvious. But of course I couldn't tell Mello and Trin why I felt like crying. Lucinda knew, though. And she was determined to help me keep up my perky front.

"Let's do charades," she said. "See if you can guess what this is."

And so the games began. Trin and Mello laughed as hard as Lucinda did. It made me sick the way they stayed all buddy-buddy with her and basically ignored me. If they only knew!

After charades, we played cards. Then we called Lamont— who had been trying to sleep. Then more games.

During an extra-loud round of Pass the Pigs, I decided Lucinda's theory might be right. Maybe it came down to how you acted. If I laughed and had fun, maybe I could fool everyone into thinking everything was okay.

Maybe I could even fool myself.

So I sang along—loud—while we finished up the "Girls Who Rock for God" song. And I managed to giggle at Trin and Lucinda as they had a dance-off—while sitting down wearing seat belts. And I didn't complain when they picked a comedy instead of a sad movie to stick in the DVD player.

We had less than an hour until we reached Seattle, anyway. At least, it should have been less than an hour.

Outside the small town of Puyallup, something went very wrong. The television and DVD player quit, and the microwave made that *beep* again.

"Did we blow a fuse?" Trin asked. "What's plugged in?"

Mello looked at the plugs. "Nothing extra. Weird."

"The air conditioner quit working too," Sandie called from the driver's seat. "I think something serious may be wrong here."

Trin looked at me.

I threw my hands in the air. "Whatever, Trin! Just try to make the failure of the electrical system my fault. I mean, yeah, I admit I got cheese on the quilt. And chocolate on your super suit. But I am not in charge of the whole—"

"Did you check the gas gauge this morning? That was on your list, right?"

"Yeah, I did it before we left. We had just over half a tank."

Mello yelled, "Harmony!"

"What? A half tank is more than enough to make it to Seattle, right? How much do we have now, Sandie?"

"A little less than a quarter tank," she answered.

"See? No worries. What does the gas tank have to do with the electrical stuff, anyway?"

Mello had her head in her hands, and Trin stared up at the ceiling, like she couldn't stand to look at me.

"You're kidding, right?" I asked. "You guys planned this just to give me a hard time, I bet."

Trin finally lowered her eyes to mine. "Harmony, the reason you're supposed to check the gas gauge is to make sure we *never* get below a quarter tank."

"Don't you remember Mr. C's speech?" Mello asked.

Something clicked in the back of my mind. "Oh, yeah. The gas tank runs the—" I stopped and swallowed. "It runs the generator."

"Which runs everything electrical," Mello added.

Trin nodded. "And if the gas gets below a quarter tank?"

I felt like a criminal in front of a firing squad. "The generator cuts off."

"Right. And getting more gas won't help," Mello said with a moan. "Oh, I can't believe this! Mr. and Mrs. C trusted us with their RV, and we ruined it."

Trin patted Mello's hand. "*We* didn't ruin it, Mello. *Harmony* ruined it. She was too busy playing games and making jokes to—"

The tears I'd been fighting all day began to fall. "If you only knew—"

Lucinda squeezed my arm in warning.

"What?" Mello asked. "If we knew what?"

Lucinda shook her head the tiniest bit.

I wiped the tears away angrily. "Nothing. Forget it."

Sandie said, "Harmony, start calling around to find the nearest RV repair shop. I hope there is one in this neck of the woods. It could be that we'll have to go hours out of our way."

"We can't," Trin reminded her. "We've got a concert in Seattle tonight."

Mello added, "Our biggest one yet. Twenty-one thousand people."

Sandie reached for a tissue and wiped her eyes. "Twenty-one thousand people hungry to hear the gospel message. We have to get you there! But I'm afraid to keep driving, girls. I don't know if we're making the damage worse." More tears. "I do feel bad for my sweet friends Renaldo and Theresa. It was so kind of them to loan their RV, and now . . ." She left that thought hanging and blew her nose.

I made about ten calls and then yelled happily, "There's a shop on the other side of Puyallup! It's only about twenty minutes out of the way." I gave Sandie directions and told the others, "It's going to be fine. We'll stop in for a few minutes, and they'll get everything working. Then we'll cruise into Seattle for our final concert."

"All's well that ends well," Lucinda quoted.

Trin said, "I hope so."

• • •

We pulled into the parking lot of the RV shop and I ran inside. I told the woman behind the counter, "We let the gas get below a quarter tank in our RV and it shut off the genera- tor and we need you to fix it fast, please, because we've got a concert in Seattle in a couple of hours."

She didn't even look up. She just peered over her tiny black glasses and typed something into her computer. "Make, model, and year?" she asked.

"Just a minute." I ran outside and got the information from Sandie then came back in and told her.

"And you let the gas get below a quarter tank?" she asked.

I nodded, but she wasn't looking at me. I forced myself to say yes.

She shook her head. "That causes some serious problems. Can cost a pretty penny too." She typed for a while, until I wondered if she'd forgotten all about me.

I cleared my throat.

She kept typing.

"It can be fixed, though, right?" I asked.

"Usually," she answered, in a voice that didn't offer much hope. "It can take a long time to clear the lines and—"

"How long?" I asked. "Our concert starts at seven. Can you get us on the road by—" I looked at the clock behind her, which read four forty-five. "By five o'clock?"

She snorted.

"Five fifteen?" I asked, desperately calculating minutes. I guessed we were forty minutes from Seattle now. "That will put us in Seattle before six. We'd have just enough time to—"

"We aren't going to be able to work on it tonight. Our repair shop is closed down for the day."

"What? Closed down?"

"We closed at four thirty."

"But when I called, you said you were open."

"Right. The office is open. The repair shop is closed."

"But—" I paced around the tiny waiting room, wishing she had chosen to share that small detail over the phone.

"What are we supposed to do, then? Where's the nearest shop that's actually open?"

"There's one about an hour and a half from here. Course, it'll be closed too by the time you get there."

I rubbed my face with both hands. "So, you can't help me? No one can help me?"

"We can help you ... tomorrow morning," she answered. "What you do is leave your RV here with us overnight. You don't want to be driving it with the generator out. We'll get on it first thing tomorrow."

"But where will we sleep tonight?" I asked. "How will we get to our concert?"

For the first time, she looked right at me. "I make appointments for RV repair. I am not a travel agent."

I started for the door but heard her mumble, "And I'm not the one who let the gas get below a quarter tank."

In the parking lot, Bob, Sandie, Lamont, Trin, Mello, and Lucinda all waited to hear the verdict.

"The good news is they can fix it," I said.

I watched them all heave a sigh of relief. Then I added, softly, "Most likely." I lifted my chin and tried to be brave as I plunged ahead.

"Unfortunately," I continued, "the repair shop is closed. We'll have to leave Old Bessie here and come back for her tomorrow."

"What?" Trin yelled.

Mello put her hands on her hips. "How are we gonna—"

"I'll call a taxi for us," I offered. "Sandie can ride in the truck with Bob, and Lamont can ride with us. Get your stuff for tonight."

"Where will we sleep?" Lucinda asked.

Mello turned to her. "Hey, don't you live in Seattle?"

"About forty-five minutes outside it, on the other side. But, yeah, if you want to—"

"No, we'll get a hotel," I said. "I'll pay for it."

Mello said, "Harmony—"

"Please. Let me do this, OK?" I asked. I got out my phone to call a taxi, but realized I had no idea what number to call. "Start packing," I told them. "I'll find us a ride."

The behind-the-counter woman was locking the door.

"Wait!" I begged. "I need a number for a taxi service."

"There aren't any taxis out here," she said through the door. "We're too far from the big city."

"But what do people do when they drop off their RVs?" I asked.

She looked as if she'd never considered that problem before. "I guess they have somebody come get 'em. I don't know. Like I said, I make appointments for RV repair. I'm not runnin' a limo service."

I felt like I could pull my hair out. We were less than an hour's drive from Seattle, where twenty-one thousand of our fans were already starting to gather, and apparently we couldn't get there to do the concert.

Because of me.

I watched through the glass doors as the woman tidied her papers and got ready to leave. On the one hand, I couldn't stand her. She certainly hadn't been overly helpful. On the other hand, I felt like if I let her leave, all hope of making it to Seattle would leave with her.

I banged on the door.

She looked up and rolled her eyes. I could tell she thought, *She's still here?*

"Please," I called. "I know it's not part of your job. But I'm desperate. Do you, maybe, know someone who's going to Seattle?"

"Seattle, you say?" she asked.

"Yes. We're supposed to do a concert in Seattle at seven o'clock tonight!" Had this woman listened to anything I'd said?

She came back to the door. "My husband is picking me up any minute now, and we're going to the waterfront farmer's market. He's got some blackberries he wants to sell. I wonder if we could fit you—"

"Yes! Yes, please!" I said.

• • •

"You're serious, Harmony?" Trin asked, looking over the peeling paint and rusty bumpers on the farmer's truck. "You want us to ride to Seattle in the back of a pickup?"

Mello looked like she wanted to throttle me. "Squeezed in between baskets of blackberries and strawberries?"

"Be glad it's not baskets of fresh fish," I said, climbing in.

Lamont smiled as he helped Trin and Mello up. "At least I won't have to listen to country music."

"What if my friends from home see me?" Lucinda asked, settling in beside me. "I told them I'd be coming in with the rock band—not with Old MacDonald."

"Then walk," I snapped. "Look, it's the best I could do under the circumstances."

"Circumstances created—let us not forget—by you, Harmony," Trin said.

"Got it," I said. "Just get in and hang on. I told him to floor it."

The farmer drove us right up to the door of the stadium, which was kind of a blessing and kind of a curse. I had to admit, I wasn't any more excited than my friends were about showing up for our grand finale in the back of a rusty truck, all windblown and grimy.

"Just smile and wave," Trin said. "Act like we did this on purpose."

Mello nodded. "Right. A publicity stunt. A very stupid publicity stunt."

"Who's in the limo?" Lucinda asked, pointing to the black stretch that pulled to the curb just as we did, about thirty feet behind us.

"I don't know. It must be someone famous," I answered. "I can't tell what the crowd is yelling."

"Get your phones out," Mello said. "Maybe, if the crowd breaks, we can get a picture."

Trin rolled her eyes. "They're yelling 'Chosen Girls.' They think it's us!"

"Oh, how I wish it were," Mello moaned.

"Hey!" I said. "Quick, while everyone is distracted—let's make a break for it!"

Lamont nodded. "Right. I've gotta unload equipment, so I'll see you chicks onstage."

I grabbed my bag, jumped out, and called, "Thanks so much!" to the farmer and the RV lady. Then I ducked my head and ran for the stadium doors.

"Good call, Harmony," Lucinda said as we pushed the doors open. "No one's even looking—"

A tall, skinny security guard stepped in front of us. "Not so fast, ladies. I need to see your tickets, please."

"But we're performing," I said. "We're the Chosen Girls."

He laughed. "Look at this, buddy. These ladies claim they're the Chosen Girls."

Another guard walked over. "Wow. Good try. You even did the pink and blue hair, huh? But we're not buying it."

Trin dug in her purse. "Look. Here's my school ID. Trinity Adams. Believe me now? Our RV broke down and we're totally late and—"

"Do you think they could be?" the first guard asked.

Just then, our faithful backstage assistant rounded the corner. "Trin! Mello! Harmony! We've been freaking out." She looked us up and down and frowned. "Let's get you cleaned up and costumed. You're on in ..." She hesitated, checking her watch. "Thirty minutes."

Trin did a frenzied search of the dressing room walls. "There are no plugs in here! How am I supposed to straighten my hair?"

"Look at mine! It's all greasy from the ride," Mello whined. "It looks worse than the time I used Latherē."

Lucinda pulled her lips back as she looked in the mirror. "I should probably floss—I think I've got gnats in my teeth."

"Forget about hair and teeth, guys. Wash your faces and let's go," I said. "At least we're at the stadium. It could be worse."

We threw on our costumes and dashed through the backstage corridor. A deep voice boomed behind us. "Harmony Gomez and Lucinda Gomez?"

I turned around and saw two uniformed policemen headed our way.

The taller one pulled out a small notepad and said, "We need to ask the two of you a few questions about an incident that took place at an RV park on Gold Beach."

I felt the heat rush to my face as Mello and Trin looked from me to the cops and back to me again. "OK," I whispered. "So it just got worse."

chapter • 11

• • •

Lucinda grabbed my hand and squeezed it. Hard. "Of course," she told the policemen. "Are you talking about the vandalism? We heard about that right before we left the campground. We'll be happy to answer any questions, but we don't know much, because our own site didn't get damaged."

The two cops looked at each other. The shorter one pointed to me with his chin. "Let's start with her."

For the first time all day, I wanted Lucinda with me. I needed her acting abilities on my side. But they pulled me away from her and led me down the corridor. As I listened to the *clump, clump, clump* of their shoes and the nervous *thump, thump, thump* of my pounding heart, I tried to prepare myself for what was coming. I'd seen TV shows, so I knew keeping my secret wouldn't be easy. One policeman (probably the tall one) would ask me the hard questions, while the other one would play the nice cop, pretending to be my buddy. Together, they would wear me down until I spilled the beans.

What then? Would they go out onstage and announce to all twenty-one thousand fans what I had done? That I couldn't perform because they were taking me to jail?

Jonah Harrison's whole campaign would be ruined. The reputation of our band would be ruined. And I'd be on my way to spending ten to twenty in the big house.

I couldn't let that happen.

Since I knew Lucinda was right about my inability to lie well, I decided I just wouldn't say anything.

Not a word.

No matter what.

They took me into a room and shut the door. They pulled three folding chairs into a circle and sat down, pointing to the third chair for me. I sat down and bowed my head, asking God to help me be strong.

He answered my prayer, but not in the way I expected.

The taller policeman spoke first. "Now, Harmony, we got a call from—"

"It's true!" I blurted out. "I'm guilty. But I didn't mean to mess everything up."

They looked at each other.

"I just wanted to have adventures, you know? The ultimate vacation."

The short one raised his eyebrows. I kept talking.

"And this is all my fault. Instead of listening when Renaldo Dear told us about the RV, I planned to get a disco ball and a chocolate fountain. And I remembered those, but I forgot

Mello's shampoo, and I feel just awful!" I started to cry, and the tall policeman handed me a tissue.

"When I lost the map, we thought we'd miss the concert, and Mello and Trin were way mad at me. Then my cousin came and we wanted to hike, so I hid the dirty dishes in the drawer. And the macaroni and salsa won't come off the quilt!"

The policemen looked confused, but I had to get it all out.

"Those mean boys said we'd only roast marshmallows, but then they went around busting people's stuff. And Lucinda said it might be fun, but it was awful. I hated it. I was so worried about it, I forgot the rules about the RV, and I broke the generator and we barely got here tonight." I stopped and blew my nose, loud. "But it doesn't matter now because you'll have to take me to prison, so the concert will have to be canceled, or—"

I cried harder as I thought of a worse option. "I guess Mello and Trin will go on without me." I sobbed out, "I just play bass. I don't even sing. They probably wouldn't ... even ... miss ... me."

The cops didn't say anything. I lifted my chin and held my hands out to them. "You can go ahead and handcuff me. But please go easy on Lucinda. She's already in trouble, and I wasn't supposed to tell. But I couldn't help it. I'm sick of pretending, and I know I deserve to be punished. I've blamed all this stuff on everyone and everything else, but it's all been my fault, hasn't it? I just want to make it right."

A knock sounded at the door, and Trin and Mello burst in. Trin looked at the policemen and said, "I don't have clue one what's going on, but we're onstage in five minutes. And the Chosen Girls just aren't the Chosen Girls without Harmony."

I wailed, "Oh, Trin! Do you really feel that way?"

"Please let her perform with us," Mello begged. "She can talk to you afterward."

The tall cop said, "Well, I think we could do that."

"Sí?" I asked. "I promise I won't try to escape."

"We'll be in the front row, watching to see that you don't," the short one said.

"OK, Harmony, what's up?" Trin asked as she, Mello, and I ran to the backstage entrance.

"Oh, amigas, I'm so sorry." I dropped my voice to a whisper as we found the assistant with the flashlight and headed into the darkened stadium. "I've made such stupid choices. I wanted this to be the ultimate vacation, but I've turned it into the ultimate disaster." We started up the steps. "I messed up your quilt, Mello, and your super suit, Trin. And more than that. And I almost ruined our chance to be here tonight and tell people about Jesus." I reached out to hug each of them before they headed to their instruments. "Forgive me, please?"

Trin nodded, taking my hand. "Sure, Harmony."

"Definitely," Mello added, squeezing my other hand in the darkness.

"One more thing," I said, not ready to let go. "Will you promise to love me, no matter what? And come visit me in jail?"

They both squeaked, "What?" Just as the announcer said, "Presenting . . . the Chosen Girls!"

The flashing colored lights came on, revealing us hanging out—not at our instruments—in the middle of the stage.

I held firmly to each of their hands and lifted them above my head in a symbol of triumph, and the crowd went wild.

I *felt* triumphant. No matter what lay before me, I was glad I had told the truth.

I prayed my way through the concert, asking God's forgiveness for the many things I'd done wrong over the course of the trip. By the time we got to "Girls Who Rock for God," I was ready to sing my heart out. Thankfully, since I wasn't miked, no one could hear me.

Except God. And I was fine with that.

Yeah, we've been blessed.
We've got the best of
A Good Book
And good hooks.
What happens next
Is in the hands of
The one whom we pray to.
And we know he's listening from above.

"I'm ready, God," I whispered, still plucking notes on my bass. "I'm glad whatever happens next is in your hands."

We went backstage for Jonah's talk, but I peeked through the curtain instead of watching on the monitor. Lucinda sat in the front row, between the two policemen, and I wanted to see her reaction. I prayed this would be the night she would get her life turned around.

Jonah spoke from the gospel of John — chapter 10 — about Jesus being the gate for the sheep. He explained that no one took Jesus' life from him. Jesus chose to lay down his life for the sheep — for us. Because he gave himself to take away our sins, Jesus is our only way to heaven.

"Thanks, Jesus," I whispered. "Thanks for doing that for me."

Lucinda sat slumped down in her seat, arms crossed, not seeming to pay attention at all. What had Aunt Berta called her? A lost sheep? I wanted to shake her and say, "Don't you see? Jesus loves you so much he died for you."

But I forgot about Lucinda as Jonah read another verse from John 10 that totally caught my attention.

> *The thief comes only to steal and kill and*
> *destroy; I have come that they may have life,*
> *and have it to the full.*

I thought about that as Jonah finished up his talk. And I still thought about it as Trin, Mello, and I went back onstage to play the final song. I picked up my bass and played softly as Jonah said, "Some of you have never asked Jesus to come into your heart and forgive you for your sins. You can do that tonight—right now. If you'd like to pray to accept God's free gift of salvation, come forward and stand here at the front of the auditorium."

People began to flood the area in front of the stage.

"Some of you are already Christians," he continued. "But you haven't been listening to your shepherd's voice. You've been listening to the world's lies instead, and it's costing you. You can come forward tonight too. Ask God to forgive you. Make a new commitment to stand firm."

I could feel my heart pounding stronger than the sound of Mello's drums. I knew he was speaking to me.

But what could I do? I had to keep playing. Besides, I had already asked God to forgive me. And what would people think if one of the members of the band went down to pray?

I struggled to keep my mind on the song as Jonah led people in the sinner's prayer. "Jesus, I admit I'm a sinner. I have willfully broken your laws. I believe you died on the cross for my sins, and I confess that you are Lord. Thank you for saving me."

I missed a note, and shook my head in frustration. What was I doing? I didn't care what people thought.

I put my guitar down and started for the steps at the front of the stage. But the area was so crowded; I knew I couldn't get a spot down there. I humbled myself completely and got down on my knees right there on the edge of the stage. I closed my eyes and shut out Mello and Trin, Lucinda and the policemen, and Jonah and the twenty-one thousand fans.

I wanted to be alone with my shepherd.

"Jesus, I love you," I whispered. "Thank you for dying so I can have life. Thank you for forgiving me, even when I make stupid choices. It's hard, God. Our world is so full of bad stuff! From now on, Jesus, no matter what people around me are doing, help me listen to your voice. Help me choose the full life you want for me."

I felt someone's hand on my back. When I opened my eyes, I was shocked to see Lucinda kneeling beside me, her long dark lashes wet with tears. "Lucinda?" I asked, glancing around us. "I didn't expect to see *you* here."

She grinned. "Yeah, I bet. But I had to come. This whole night was like – I don't know – like Jonah was talking just to me."

"I didn't think you were listening," I admitted.

A giggle escaped her lips. "Well, I've been working on my 'I'm bored out of my skull' look for a long time now. But it doesn't mean nothing's getting through."

"So you really heard what Jonah said? About Jesus giving up his life for you?"

"I heard it," she answered. "And I've known it for a while now. But I didn't want to give everything up. I wanted to make my own choices, do things my own way, you know?"

I took her hand. "Yeah, I know."

She jerked her head toward the two cops in the front row. "Maybe I'm starting to figure out my own way isn't exactly brilliant."

I nodded in agreement.

"Anyway, I wanted to come pray," she said, "but I was too afraid ... until you laid down your guitar and knelt on the stage. I knew if you could do that, I had to be brave too." She nodded her head toward the floor of the stadium. "Sorry I took so long. It wasn't easy getting through that crowd."

I reached for her hand. "Lucinda, I'm so sorry. I wanted to be a good influence on you. Instead I messed everything up."

She shook her head slowly. "No, Harmony, it was my fault. I wanted you to think I was cool. I've been trying to prove that to everyone for a long time now—most of all to myself. I do crazier and crazier stuff, hoping something will fill that empty place inside me. But I haven't found anything that does."

I put my arm around her. "That's because only Jesus can fill that hole," I explained. "Like the verse Jonah read. 'I have come that they may have life, and have it to the full.'"

"That's what I want," Lucinda said. "Do you think it's too late, you know, to pray that sinner's prayer?"

"I'm sure it's not too late," I answered.

•••

The stadium was almost empty by the time Lucinda and I made our way back to the policemen.

"We just got a call from Gold Beach," the tall one said. "Four boys there originally told police they saw the two of you vandalizing the campground. They finally admitted the two of you were present, but they actually did the damage."

"So that means —," I began.

"Well, normally you would be punished just as if you had done the crime. If you're there when it happens, it doesn't matter if you actually participate or not. A good reason to be careful who you hang around," the short policeman explained. "But the boys insisted they were to blame, and so the campground manager has decided not to press charges against the two of you." He smiled at us. "So we won't need to handcuff you after all. But I hope, after this, you'll make better choices."

I hugged Lucinda. "Absolutely, sir," I promised. "Both of us will be making better choices from now on."

•••

The next morning we all cried — I thought maybe even Lamont wiped away a tear — as we hugged Lucinda good-bye. And — get this — Aunt Berta bawled her head off, thanking me for being a "good influence" on her daughter. I didn't know whether I should laugh or cry about that.

Back at the RV shop, my friend, the behind-the-counter woman, filled us in. "Air got in your lines. That's what happens with these diesels when you let the gas get below a quarter tank. Had to clean 'em out completely. Not a simple job, let me tell you. But you're fixed up now. Good as new. Here's your bill."

I gasped when I saw the amount: two thousand, seven hundred dollars.

"I'll pay it," I volunteered. I looked at Trin, Mello, and Lamont. "If we can use money from the band's account, I promise I'll work until I've paid back every penny."

They nodded, and Lamont said, "That's very responsible of you, Harmony."

Trin added, "Ohwow. *Responsible* and *Harmony* — those are two words you never expected to use in the same sentence."

"Trin!" Mello exclaimed. "That was way harsh."

"I'll take it as a compliment to the new, improved Harmony," I said with a wink. "And once we're on the road, Mello, I think you've got some homework I promised to help you with."

She laughed. "Right. You take care of the paperwork on the RV, and I'll get my stuff out. Trin, Lamont, come help me."

I didn't see why she needed so much help getting out one silly worksheet, but I stayed behind with Bob and Sandie until we got everything signed. It took like forever.

When I finally opened the door to the RV, I stood frozen in surprise. Chosen Girls music blasted as the disco light threw flecks of rainbows on every surface. And on the counter, stemware glasses of cider stood next to the flowing chocolate fountain.

"What's this?" I asked. "I thought we were doing Greek and Roman history."

"We will," Mello promised. "But first we're going to celebrate something a little more recent. Jonah Harrison called."

Trin's smile was amazingly big and bright—even for her. "According to those little cards they asked people to fill out, thirteen thousand people got saved during our 'Anything but Coasting' tour."

"Can you even wrap your mind around that?" Lamont asked, handing me a glass. "That's a lot of folks."

I couldn't wrap my mind around it—not all at once. But I could understand Lucinda—her need and the help she had found. And I could understand the same thing happening for person after person until it added up to thousands and thousands who didn't have to feel empty anymore—who now knew God loved them, and had a full life planned for them.

"Thirteen thousand! That's a pretty good start, isn't it?" I asked.

Mello looked confused. "Start? Harmony, the campaign is over."

I felt a grin spread across my face. "Our first campaign is over," I corrected. "The first of many!"

Trin and Lamont laughed.

"I mean, that was just the West Coast," I continued. "What about the East Coast? The Midwest? And don't forget Europe, Africa, and Asia!"

Mello shook her head. "Harmony, do you ever stop?"

"Not when there are amazing places to see, adventures to be had, and souls to save," I answered.

Trin grabbed a glass and winked at Mello. "I guess we'll have to drink this stuff all by ourselves. Harmony's too busy planning to celebrate."

"No way!" I argued, reaching for a strawberry. "I'm always ready to celebrate."

I held the fruit under the flowing chocolate, and then carried it and my cider to the couch. I propped my feet up on the table as I hummed along with the music. Then I started to laugh. "This *so* did not turn out to be the vacation I planned. But isn't God good? He managed to turn it into the ultimate tour after all!"

CHOSEN GIRLS

CHECK OUT
this excerpt
from book one in the
Chosen Girls series.

GOD rock

BACKSTAGE PASS

zonderkidz

Created by Beth Michael
Written by Cheryl Crouch

chapter • 1

• • •

wednesday

My school had those flaky elections at the end of last year.
You know, Most Beautiful This, Cutest That? Makes me sick.

Not just because I didn't get on the ballot, either. I can deal.
But school is competitive enough without making it official.

I do know one election I could win. If the ballot said Least
Likely to Become a Rock-Star Superhero, you'd see my name,
Melody McMann, checked on everyone's list. Definitely.

I'm not lame or anything. I'm just quiet and reserved. On
a good day, I like to think of myself as chic. On a bad day,
boring seems to fit better.

That's why it's even more bizarre that it happened. The
whole rock-star – superhero thing.

I know. A month ago I wouldn't have believed it, either.

• • •

I stood balanced on tiptoe on the arm of the old couch in the shed. I could barely reach the ceiling. I had to stretch to hold the nail and hammer above my head.

Tap. Tap. Tap.

The nail didn't even scratch the ceiling. The fabric I wanted to nail up felt heavy, and my hands were numb. My arms ached from doing more physical work in the last couple weeks than I usually did in a year.

I grunted in frustration.

"I could do that," my neighbor Lamont said for the third time. He sat at the drums, banging away. His dark, skinny arms were a blur. His super-short black curly hair shone with sweat from his efforts.

Lamont's an okay guy, but he's kind of a dork. I'd never have let him in the shed if I hadn't been desperate for company.

And seeing him at the drums — it always made me remember a different boy. One who could actually play.

Lamont stopped b g a said, "You might as well let me. You're messing   hm, anyway."

"As if you have a   to mess up!" I mumbled.

Lamont pretend   urt. "I've taken two years of lessons, woman!"

It always cracks me up when he calls me "woman."

I turned to climb down. "Yeah, I remember when you started. Maybe it's time to move on. You might try —" I began, and then, boom! I fell off the couch and splatted face-first on the floor. My head missed the still-open can of buttercream semigloss paint by less than three inches.

"That's it. Give me the stuff you're hanging up," Lamont said. I felt him take the material, hammer, and nails from my clenched hands. He stepped over my still-splatted body.

BANG! BANG! BANG!

"First nail's in. You want this stuff across the whole back of the room, right?" he asked. I heard him work his way across the shed.

"Really, Lamont, don't panic," I said into the carpet. "I know it looks like a serious injury, but I'll be OK." I lifted my head and peeked up at him through my hair.

"That's a relief, Mello." He didn't even glance at me. "What's with the extreme garage makeover? You've about killed yourself painting this place."

I sighed and pushed up onto my elbows. "It's a surprise for Harmony. I'm trying to give the shed some style. Isn't it nifty? I'm going to hang up those prints too. I can't wait to see her face when she walks in!"

"When's she back?"

"Today! But I don't know what time. She's been gone forever! This is the longest we've been apart since second grade."

"Two weeks, right?"

"Two and a half. Almost three."

"Whatever. All I know is when Harmony gets back, then for sure Lamont's kicked out of the shed."

He had that right. Definitely.

BANG! BANG! BANG!

"I'm done."

"Thanks, Lamont," I said. "For a computer geek, you're pretty handy with the hammer. Maybe we'll even let you hang sometimes. We do have a whole month to kill before school starts."

A month! No more camps or vacations. Just me and Harmony, chilling out. Together.

I looked at the ocean-blue cloth. It hung like a curtain across the room, covering up my parents' tools and junk. The matching pillows looked great on the tan couch.

The shed had always been a decent hangout, but now it looked like something in a magazine. I could hardly tell I was in the garage. It could pass for an apartment or a living room.

"Think she'll like it?"

Lamont smiled. "Yeah. But she'd probably rather have purple checks and stripes."

That's true. Harmony and I don't have much in common when it comes to style. We don't have much in common, period. That's what makes our friendship so much fun.

My cell phone rang with the tune of "La Bamba." I pulled it out of my pocket.

"Harmony!" I sang into the phone.

"Hello, Mello!" she shouted.

"Where are you?" I asked. I held the phone a few inches from my ear, like I always do when I talk to Harmony. Otherwise, I get a headache.

"I'm home!"

"Excellent!"

"Sí! Can I come over?"

"Definitely! I'm dying to see you."

"Cool frijoles. It's been hundreds of years! Meet me halfway?"

I looked at the stack of art prints. "Uh … I'm kinda working on something. Do you mind just meeting me at the shed?"

"Give me fifteen minutes," she said and hung up.

I scrambled up and grabbed a botanical print off the coffee table. Very elegant.

"She's home, Lamont! Harmony's back! She's coming in fifteen minutes! Hurry! Help me get this artwork hung."

He started nailing. "You recovered pretty fast," he commented.

"Just be quiet and help me. I want this place perfect when she gets here."

Turns out, I didn't need to rush. After helping me hang pictures, hide paint cans, and touch up the trim, Lamont left. As he headed out he said, "I'm outie. Tell Harmony 'hey' for me. You two will wanna do that girl talk stuff, anyway." For a guy, Lamont has a decent amount of brains.

Half an hour after he left, I was still wandering around fluffing pillows and rearranging magazines. I figured Harmony had gotten stuck doing the family thing. She has a huge family.

I went crazy waiting. We live only three blocks apart. Of course, the blocks are long blocks. What could possibly happen to someone walking alone . . .

What could happen? I thought. Oh, no. All kinds of terrible things could happen. What was I thinking? Why hadn't I called?

I whipped out my cell phone and clicked on her cross-eyed picture. Her phone rang three times. I tried to prepare myself for the worst. Maybe a scary voice saying, "I have Harmony. Put five thousand dollars in small bills inside a black briefcase—"

"Hello, Mello!"

"Harmony?"

"Yeah. Oh, no! I should have called. I'm so sorry. I've been, um . . . listen. I'm coming now, OK, and I'm going to surprise you."

I realized I'd been holding my breath and exhaled. Then I looked around the shed again and grinned. "And I'm going to surprise you too!" I said.

"Great. Be right there."

I sat down and drummed a beat on the coffee table.

Finally, I heard a knock.

I ran over (tripping only once) and flung the door open.

And I froze.

The tall girl with the mass of hot-pink hair and the perfect smile couldn't be Harmony. Definitely not.

I had never seen this girl in my life.

Chosen Girls is a dynamic new series that communicates a message of empowerment and hope to Christian youth who want to live out their faith. These courageous and compelling girls stand for their beliefs and encourage others to do the same. When their cross-cultural outreach band takes off, Trinity, Melody, and Harmony explode onto the scene with style, hot music, and genuine, age-relatable content.

Backstage Pass

Book One • Softcover • ISBN 0-310-71267-X

In *Backstage Pass*, shy, reserved Melody gets her world rocked when a new girl moves in across the street from her best friend, Harmony. Soon downtime—or any time with Harmony at all—looks like a thing of the past as the strong-willed Trinity invades Melody and Harmony's world and insists that the three start a rock band.

Available now at your local bookstore!

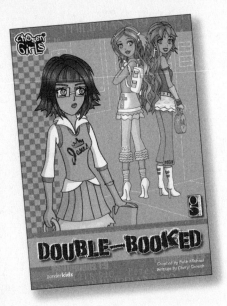

Double-Booked

Book Two • Softcover • ISBN 0-310-71268-8

In *Double-Booked*, Harmony finds
that a three-way friendship is challenging,
with Trinity befriending a snobby clique
and Melody all negative. Through a
series of mistakes, Harmony unwittingly
unites the two against her and learns that
innocent comments hurt more than you
think. Ultimately, the Chosen Girls
are united again in time to sing for
a crowd that really needs to hear
what they have to say.

Unplugged

Book Three • Softcover • ISBN 0-310-71269-6

The band lands a fantastic opportunity to
travel to Russia, but the "international tour,"
as they dub it, brings out Trinity's take-charge
personality. Almost too confidently, she
tries to control fundraising efforts and the
tour to avoid another mess by Harmony. But
cultural challenges, band member clashes,
and some messes of her own convince Trinity
she's not really in charge after all. God is. And
his plan includes changed lives, deepened
faith, and improved relationships with
her mom and friends.

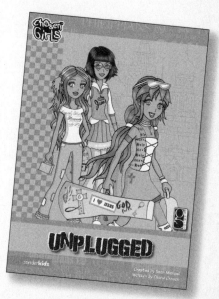

Solo Act

Book Four • Softcover • ISBN 0-310-71270-X

Melody needs some downtime—and the summer youth retreat will really hit the spot! But a last-minute crisis at camp means an opportunity for the band to lead worship every morning, plus headline the camp's big beach concert and go to camp for free. Too busy and unhappy, Melody makes some selfish choices that result in the girls getting lost, sunburned, in trouble, and embarrassed. Can she pull out of the downward spiral before she ruins camp—and the band—completely?

Big Break

Book Five • Softcover • ISBN 0-310-71271-8

The Chosen Girls are back! As opportunities for the band continue to grow, Harmony can't resist what she sees as a big break ... and what could be better than getting signed by an agent?

Available now at your local bookstore!

Sold Out

Book Six • Softcover • ISBN 0-310-71272-6

Dedicated to proving herself to others, Trinity gets involved in organizing the school talent show. Before she knows it, she accepts a dare from Chosen Girls' rival band to be decided by the outcome of a commercial audition.

Overload

Book Seven • Softcover • ISBN 0-310-71273-4

Melody discovers a latent talent for leadership that she never knew she had. When she begins a grief recovery group for kids like her, she loses her focus on the work God is doing through the Chosen Girls.

We want to hear from you. Please send your comments
about this book to us in care of zreview@zondervan.com. Thank you.

ZONDERVAN.com/
AUTHORTRACKER
follow your favorite authors